Raleigh Review

Literary & Arts Magazine

VOL. 16.1

SPRING 2026

RALEIGH REVIEW
VOL. 16.1 SPRING 2026

Raleigh Review, Vol. 16, No. 1, Spring 2026

501(c)(3) Co-Incorporators:
Will Badger & Rob Greene
Raleigh Review, the organization officially established with the
Internal Revenue Service and the NC Secretary of State on 21 May 2010

Raleigh Review, the magazine founded as *RIG Poetry*
February 21, 2010 | Robert Ian Greene

Cover image "Drill Baby Drill" by Taylor Stoneman
Cover design by Alexis Olson

ISBN: 978-1-59498-229-3

Raleigh Review is printed and bound via Fernwood Press in Oregon, U.S.A. and
distributed globally via Ingram.

Raleigh Review, PO Box 6725, Raleigh, NC 27628
Visit: raleighreview.org

RALEIGH
REVIEW

table of contents

FICTION

fiction cont.

POETRY

poetry cont.

illustrations

contributors

RALEIGH REVIEW

VOL. 16.1 SPRING 2026

FROM THE EDITOR

BY THE TIME you're reading this issue of *Raleigh Review,* spring will be sprung, at least in the Carolinas. If the almanac can be trusted, we've had our last frost. The irises are in the middle of their bloom. It's time for me to break off and plant a few more pads from the spineless prickly pear I hauled three years ago from my mom's yard in Texas. There I am digging a hole, wiping my forehead with a muddy hand and pulling at my shirt, saying something we always say, like, "It's not the heat. It's this humidity."

But right now, as I write this and as our materials for this issue are due, it's January. There's a serious and some are saying dangerous winter storm looming over much of the country, even the south. Forecasters are predicting ice for our region. The Walmart is sold out of bread and bottled water. There's lots of talk about generators, the grid, firewood. Students are already asking if classes will be canceled.

We've only just started a new semester, but the first assignments are coming up due, and you can feel the resolve waning. I try not to let on how much I relate. The new year doesn't feel so new anymore. A couple of weeks ago, hopes high, I bought one of those journals, the kind that makes you realize that not only are you ungrateful, you're also incapable of what promises to be a very simple task of writing a couple of sentences a day. Each page is a list of prompts and blanks that should take you about five minutes to complete, and still it's too much. I did it three times, I think. January 1-3. The journal predicted I would falter. I see that now in the way the pages are left undated.

Under the date line, there are three more lines to list what you're grateful for and another blank for your favorite moment of the day. And even though I've only written three times, I've got to say, the journal had an impact. I often find myself identifying my favorite moment. Today's was talking with a neighbor through his screen door, him stepping outside to hear me, he said, over his TV. If I were to go back to the journal, I'd write about that, the way we hollered about hats and blessings and the summer that is sure to come eventually.

But I want to tell you about another favorite moment, one that happened a week or so ago.

The thing they don't tell you about having a one-year-old is that they want to do things they can't do and because of this, it's hard sometimes to keep them entertained, especially when you're trying not to let them watch TV, and especially when—like now in January—it's cold outside. You find yourself doing weird things like writing and performing songs about the Fisher Price farmer and his cow friend. You find yourself concerned about the lack of enthusiastic applause you're sure you've earned for this original composition, and you return to the song to revise it yet again before the next performance that oddly leaves you a little weak in the knees. You think you probably haven't written enough about the cow. That's the problem. This is just one of the weird things you do on a cold afternoon in January.

You also go on what you call nature walks, which are really quick trips to the front porch where you call stray cats and wave at strangers and try to guess what color car will pass next before you get cold and have to go back inside.

It was on one of these outings that the baby surprised me. She reached up and grabbed ahold of the wind chime's clapper, and something magical happened. She was looking up at the chimes and me, her face cracking into a grin, amazed at the sound, and the sun was afternoon sun—as bright as the sun gets and brighter still for all the leaves that are gone from the trees—so bright, it made me see white spots, tiny orbs dancing around the both of us, and the baby, laughing now, doing everything for the first time, rang the chimes, and the sun and suns spun around us, and I think you could say there was something spiritual about it, this moment.

Maybe you've had an experience like that, something that shook you when and probably because you least expected it, when you were just trying to get some air and keep the dang TV off. That was my favorite moment of that day, and if I had the wherewithal, I would have written it down in that awful journal, but here in this note is a pretty good home for it too.

I left out part of the story. Those chimes were a gift from a friend, a "thinking of you" kind of gift after my mom passed away. And there was something about that moment—with the baby and the chimes—that held all three of us in a million suns, each one brighter than you could imagine. It was a kind of coming together, a falling into place.

My mom was a creative person. It's recently occurred to me that one of the hardest things about her being gone is that there's no more of her art. No more of her drawings, her paintings, her collages, the way she arranged cool old things on a mantle. I think it's in her art where I felt her energy the most. I wouldn't have known that before. But I know it now. I miss it now. It makes me even more grateful—take that, journal with all your mean blanks—to be a small part of the art we collect and produce here at *RR*.

This magazine, every issue of it, is its own collection of creative energy, its own miracle of coming together that starts, as so many things do, with a writer or an artist sitting in front of a blank page and daring themselves to get something down. They share it with us here at *RR*, and now we get to share it with you, reader. You're here now too, and we're so glad and—yes—grateful to see you. ◆

Landon Houle, editor-in-chief

NELLE YYON

CABIN 2G

Each cabin has a prayer closet. A quiet room
the size of a confessional, paneled in pine, but with no window

to church representatives. Another camper and I rename the prayer closet
the fart closet and use it daily while pretending to pray.

One afternoon, we canoe out to cliffs that jut twenty feet above
the lake and taunt one another to jump. A girl named Temple

hits the water tailbone first and crumples like a marionette. She cries out
to God until the camp nurse arrives. Sitting too painful, Temple kneels

on a rolled-up beach towel in the mess hall; during services, she lies prone
on the floor. The next morning, our camp director names her

in his breakfast prayer, praises her rejection of painkillers.
Her radiant attitude and thrice daily prayer closet visits.

We applaud after *amen* and march to archery, then riflery, then beadwork
in two rows of twelve girls each, matching shirts tucked in.

Camp songs echo off rocks and trees as we trudge to Pelican Lake
where Fridays at golden hour, campers choose Jesus

in the brisk water, joyful for rebirth. Temple is among them,
her eyes closed, arms raised, purified. Rock-cut feet bleeding in the shallows.

Her smile so bright, you could almost ignore her limp. Later, in the shower,
she whimpers, unable to dress. Her back is purple, greening at her ribs.

Temple calls to me, yanks the shower curtain closed behind us.
I pull her jeans up slowly and she gasps when denim grazes her hipbones.

She tightens her grip on my shoulders
as I button her button.

FLASH FICTION CONTEST WINNER

ELIZABETH ROSEN

MAW MAW'S CHEESE BALLS

EVERYONE LOVED Maw Maw's Cheese Balls, but that didn't stop us from wanting her to die. In a foolish act of sentimentality, Aunt Sally Ann had taken the five-by-seven recipe card from its flower-decorated box and made the famous Cheese Balls, and now the untouched platter of pimento cheese balls rolled in crushed Special K cereal sat on the sad, scratched coffee table in the living room where we all were gathered, waiting for Maw Maw to finally pass.

The air conditioner rumbled low and ugly in one of the windows. Under the scent of warm cheese, the room smelled like mildew from the water that dripped into an empty Crisco tub that sat below the unit. Still, the rug was damp in that area and, sensing this, we all pulled our chairs as far away from there as possible. It had only been days, but it felt like forever, this vigil for Maw Maw, waiting for her to get this dying thing done when she was usually efficient and brusque in her doing of things. We wanted to remember her that way, capable and sharp, even those of us who had no particular fondness for the old lady.

Aunt Susan was tucked tightly into the corner of the couch, knitting needles clicking and clacking. Her lips were pressed together into a thin, angry line, and this was because her sweet youngest sister had dared to violate Maw Maw's sacrosanct recipe box, had the audacity to think she could recreate their mother's cooking. We all knew that if there was a way to take something the wrong way, Aunt Susan would find it.

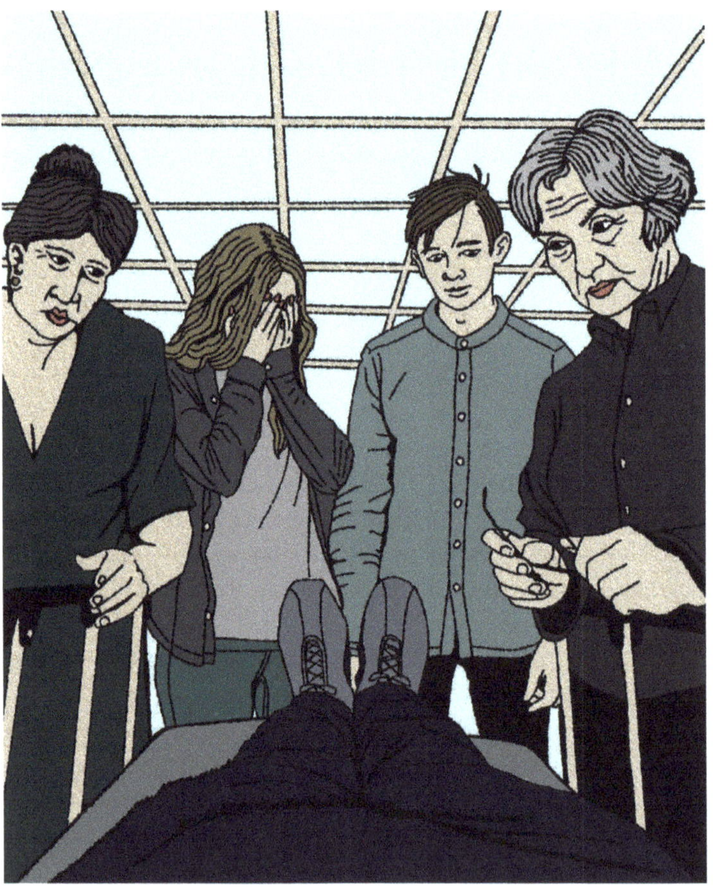

In the outdated kitchen, my father and Uncle Mort were speaking in low tones. They'd asked Uncle Joden if he wanted to join them, but Joden had looked to Susan for permission and when none had been given, he'd shaken his head and stayed seated at the opposite end of the couch from his wife. From what I could tell, if that man could have shrunk up and slipped between the seat cushions to disappear, he would have. That, from what I could gather from my parents' late-night discussions, Susan would have given permission for.

The younger children had been sent outside to play, but us older ones were expected to keep watch with the grown-ups, and my cousins and I were stationed in whatever empty spaces there were in the room. I propped my chin on my fist and watched the little ones out the window. They'd dragged an unused tire to the center of the yard and were collecting sticks and twigs to pile inside.

When the bedroom door opened and my red-eyed mother came out, I uncrossed my ankles and looked to her. She exchanged a glance with Sally Ann and shook her head sadly. The clicking of Aunt Susan's knitting needles grew louder and angrier.

My mother's gaze moved to Susan, exasperated at first, but after taking in her tightly wound elder sister, my mother's expression evolved into something closer to pity. She went to sit next to Susan, who refused to look up from her knitting. My mother reached out one hand, rough from gathering eggs and carrying pails of slop to the pigs. She lay it gently atop Susan's needles to still them. Susan stared at the now-silent needles in her lap and burst into tears.

All us kids sat up straight in our seats in shock. We looked to Joden, but Joden, too, looked bewildered as Susan lay her head against my mother's shoulder and began to openly weep. Sweet, pudgy Sally Ann came over and crouched on the floor in front of her sisters. She grasped their hands and began to cry as well. My father and Uncle Mort came from the kitchen and stood helpless in the doorway.

"Oh," Susan said, wiping her sleeve roughly against her face as if she'd lost patience with herself, "take those damn Cheese Balls and bring 'em out to the babies." It was unclear to whom this order was directed, but after a moment, I rose and took up the platter. As I pushed open the screen door, I looked back at my aunts and mother, a triad of misery caught between anticipation and grieving. The sound of their sobs drifted out to the little ones, and the children looked up in concern, but I pulled the door shut behind me and muted the sound.

I carried the platter over to where they were sitting in the dirt, patting the sticks down into the center of the tire. They raised their little faces to me, curious about the offering I'd brought, but also perhaps wondering if they were about to get in trouble for their dirty nails and sweaty cheeks. Silently, I knelt in the dirt next to them and held out the platter. Little fingers reached for the snack, a poor substitute for their grandmother's Cheese Balls, but the only one they'd ever remember now. ◆

REBECCA PYLE

AT THE BARRE

We are at the barre, it is time
for the old woman with me
to learn dance. I show her how
the colors of cement are not different than
the feel of moving this limb or that,
holding it, turning it, waiting for the rush of declaration
coming from moves made. We lean our heads low, feel
hair on our heads moving, make servants of feet.
Afterward, the grateful wordlessness. New thoughts
about the ways our bodies have found statements.
I remember Ohio, she eventually says, I remember Ohio's trees
near Newcomerstown. Moonlight in Alaska on all the snow.
The way all of you looked on your horses I rented for you.
How angry all the cars seemed in Jersey; New York nearby,
all their wandering anger. The sun baked you slow in California.
In Kansas the feeling of meadows closing around you,
growing inward and sealing you in, the intense relief of
built buildings holding off meadows.
Virginia the declarative patriarch, making you small.
Up above Canada, which I cannot return to. Mexico below
laughing at you. I remember Wyoming, how it kept pushing
us on, cars took us everywhere, my father drilled for oil
and the tall Indian in full old dress at the filling station—
remember I gave him a ride with us into another town,
and he said nothing. Watched us. Pitied us.
We had no dance.

FLASH FICTION CONTEST FINALIST

RILEY MAYES

THE VOLE

MY SISTERS found it first. They came running into the house, announcing breathlessly what they had seen. Mom told us to stay away because it might be diseased, but when she wasn't looking, I slipped outside. I found it lying on the doormat: the slim gray husk, prostrate on the 'O' of 'Welcome.' Its bone-thin paw was extended as if it meant to go farther, like it was pleading. I thought I could see its life wisping away in tiny white waves. Later, Mom said animals do this when they're close to death, present themselves. For help? I asked. No, she said. For someone to witness. ◆

SEAN CHO A.

LONG AFTERNOON

There are many other ways
this could have gone
a synthetic beat plays on
the mobile speaker
as the boy skates through
the boardwalk.
it sounds real: the voice
singing into the microphone
the tippy taps from the drum
stick testing out
the snare the piano keys
ironically just off tune.

it drifts out of ear shot:
the song: the boy with
no responsibilities in both
directions. of course
you want to live like this:
timeless with no one
wanting you to come home.

FLASH FICTION CONTEST FINALIST

RYAN PEED

PLAYING DEAD (OR DYING)

THE KEY is to be absolutely still. Unless you're actively dying. Then, you panic, thrash, scream, seize for a bit, spasm one leg, go limp, and die.

And then there are the times when only your neck is broken. Your body sprawls across the waxy floor, illuminated by the crawling glare of an enormous disco ball. Wedged between loudspeakers, your head cocks where the vertebrae are comminuted. You ignore the words blasting in your ears—you cannot scream, you cannot shout, you cannot let it all out—as the wheels on your roller skates continue to spin, tickling the soles of your feet.

This is the birthday boy's doing, of course. Those fish-belly calves crossing the slit between the speaker and the floor. Effortless coolness, skating backward like that.

He hasn't noticed me yet. Nobody has. Maybe because I'm only here because his mom made him invite the whole class, and because my mom said she would take away my rocks if I didn't go. She's so stupid. I know those rocks aren't really my friends. It's just a thing I do sometimes. I pretend dead things are alive. And I pretend alive things are dead. Or dying. And, since I have no real friends, I'm usually the alive thing I'm pretending is dead (or dying).

Most of the time, though, I hate pretending I'm dying. I'm already dying naturally, so why pretend? But then there are times when pretending to die sounds pretty great. Take right now, for example.

Birthday Boy rounds the curve. His calves are huge, sweaty, veiny. Hairy? I'm intrigued, but paralyzed. He rolls by, and I'm too distracted by the glimpse of pale legs up his grease-stained jorts to notice his path. He topples backward over my knee, then spends the next several seconds falling, his wheels *click-clacking* atop the concrete until his body finally unfurls with a loud and bony *smack.* I hold my breath. My neck is broken, but I need to turn my head. To see him up close. To know if we have something in common, now.

"Seriously, Ashley?" he shouts. "People are skating!"

My cheeks flare as he *click-clacks* away. He knows my name. But there are so many Ashleys. Three in my class alone. Birthday Boy likes Kristens and Jordans. Or maybe just Kristens and his Jordan shoes, because there are no girl Jordans in my grade. He probably made a lucky guess. I wish my name was Jordan.

"Hey." The voice is bassy and imposing, like my dad's after I disassemble his entire collection of Lego TIE Fighters. "Get up."

I lie still. I can't get up, I say without speaking. My neck is broken.

Two rough hands latch around my ankles. "You can't lie here," the voice says. "You'll hurt someone for real."

I'm dying, I say.

My lodged head resists his first attempt, so he pulls again, harder, and keeps pulling, until I'm certain he'll rip my head off, and then he grunts and I'm free. I watch my classmates skate as he drags me across the rink like I'm a mop. Not like—sometimes, you just *are* the thing, and right now that thing is a really dry mop. The smooth concrete switches to stubby carpet that raises my shirt and scratches my back. Parents and children twist in their chairs or stand to spectate across tabletops covered in bright-red plastic. Birthday Boy's mom stares into her lap, massaging her temples.

My heels hit the floor. "Get up," he commands.

My toes split and fall to each side.

He sighs. "You're *fine.*"

I'm not fine, I correct him. Dying is what I am. Dying is what he is, too. Doesn't he know? Maybe he forgot. My grandpa forgets things, too. He's almost dead. Sometimes, he acts like he's not, so I have to remind him. Maybe that's the key to a happy life: pretend you're not dying until you forget you're pretending. If that's true, what's the key to forgetting? Someday, I'll know this too. I'll know everything, and skate backward with ease.

"I *saw* you, dummy."

I lie there, paralyzed, for a moment longer. Parents return to their kids; kids return to their pizzas and claw machines. In the corner of my eye, a depressing old man with a *Manager* pin reaches for my ankles. I get up, frown at him, and skate away. ◆

JEREMIAH MORIARTY

PORTAL FANTASY

Nobody knows what Minnesota looks like.
A hand traces an arc over your shoulder,
that ridge you wish was broader. Vaster.
When you show a man
a book of Grant Wood paintings,
he says the landscapes are empty.
The familiar hand that traced your shoulder
now reaches across the curled hairs on your belly.
You lean into its embrace. Its pull.
It always seemed especially cruel
that the Pevensies lived a decade in Narnia
before they were recalled into childhood.
As a little boy you opened such portals
between worlds, circles in the rough
trading one place for another.
You never got around to closing them.

FLASH FICTION CONTEST FINALIST

CLAIRE MARIE TORN

GOOD DRIVER

HER FRIEND CRICKET lived in Washington Heights. Around 6 p.m., Lotus walked to the 23rd Street subway station. At 42nd, she switched to the A and rode the train up to 181st.

Cricket opened the door and the two girls embraced. They were twenty now and had been friends since they were fifteen. They met in high school, in the girls' bathroom, where they had complained about the same thing: everyone was boring and nobody understood them.

"I got the goods," Lotus announced.

Cricket's parents were out of town.

Lotus opened her pale blue purse. Inside was a black Bluetooth speaker, a tray of pink eyeshadow, and a little purple rock wrapped in a small plastic baggie. She had scored the MDMA from a student in her mom's acting class.

Kept inside the bag, Lotus crushed the purple rock with the back of a spoon and pressed on it, until the rock was now a pile of sharp lilac dust.

"This stuff hasn't been stepped on," Lotus said.

"I have lollipops!" Cricket replied.

"I was told it won't make you grind your teeth."

"We'll find out."

From the bathroom, Cricket retrieved a slim roll of toilet paper and ripped out two small patches. Lotus tapped out a small amount of the powder onto each of the patches. Cricket opened a bottle of white wine, and Lotus wrapped the powder in each patch. She held one out to Cricket. They swallowed the little pouches each with a swallow of Pinot Grigio.

Within forty-five minutes, they were feeling it. A rush of euphoria. They painted their faces with the pink eye shadow and danced to Depeche Mode with yellow scarves wrapped around their waists. They held hands and rubbed their sweaty fingers together, sharing stories and complaints about the boys who let them down.

"I forgive them all," Lotus said.

"Love you, girly!"

At midnight, Lotus had to go home. Her ten-year-old black poodle Gem was waiting for her. She regretted not bringing her. Her parents were also out of town.

It was January and lightly snowing. The kind of snow that covered the pavement for only a snapshot of time. Lotus had always relied on the subway, but Cricket had a discount from Uber and said, "My treat."

Outside of Cricket's building, Lotus opened the door to a silver Lexus and climbed in. The driver was a young man, probably ten years older, with an accent she couldn't place when he said hello. The backseat was very clean and smelled like incense. He had a picture taped on the sun visor of a smiling woman and young girl.

Lotus's phone was dead and she asked the driver if he had a charger. He fed her the cord and placed her phone on top of the glove compartment. She didn't think anything of it. She was still rolling. As they cruised down the West Side Highway, she was focused on the light snow that hit the windows. Her hot cheek pressed against the cold glass, eyes tilted up to the sky. She felt so warm, so open. So happy. The driver had the radio on, 90.7. She knew the song. "Pale Shelter" by Tears for Fears. Lotus asked him to turn it up.

"You like to party, huh?"

"Yeah, dude," Lotus said.

He asked if she had a boyfriend.

"Sometimes," she said truthfully.

Grooving to the song, she was immersed in the interior of backseat, its smooth leather that she sank her shoulder blades into. Even when it was twenty degrees out, she never wore tights. She didn't realize that her silk skirt was hitched up, her navy blue panties peeking out. She wasn't paying attention to the way the driver was looking at her through his rearview mirror.

Lotus pulled down her skirt when she noticed that he missed the turn that would take her home. "Where are we going?" she asked. He didn't answer. "Can I have my phone?" He still did not answer. He turned off the highway at 14th Street and went down a deserted side street. He stopped the car. Lotus tried the door, but it was locked. The driver climbed in the backseat and placed one hand on her collarbone and the other on her bare thigh. For a moment, she just looked at him. She recalled what she was told in a college class she took for gym credit. The class was called RAD for Rape Aggression Defense. "Look your attacker in the eyes, right into his eyeballs," she remembered the instructor saying. "You'll be able to read his mind." So she stared into the driver's medium sized pupils, wondering what he saw in her dilated ones. His eyes were the color of maple syrup, and in them she saw hesitation. He had never done this before.

"I don't want this," she said. Her voice remained calm, polite. Like she was talking to a friendly neighbor. "You don't want this either. I promise." She moved closer to him. "You're a good driver." She threw her arms around him, hugging him. He gently let her go.

Silently, he climbed back into the driver's seat and handed her phone back. He unlocked the door. "Thank you!" she called when she slammed it shut.

Walking up Ninth Avenue in the light snow, Lotus kept turning her head. The streets were empty. She skipped home to 21st Street.

When she got home, she hugged her little dog. After she walked her, she called Cricket.

"You must be a witch," Cricket said. "Maybe it's those red candles we lit that saved you."

She was convinced that it was the MDMA that saved her.

Maybe it was the MDMA that caused this.

She didn't know. Still high, she stayed awake, playing to the same radio channel the driver had on, wondering if he was hearing what she was listening to. ◆

ABHISHEK MEHTA

QUIET MUSIC

This morning I called my mother from work
and my father picked up.
For a moment I was stunned.
He didn't have a mobile phone,
didn't even know how to answer a call,
but there he was, telling me she was brushing her teeth.
I managed, "Oh okay. I'll call later."
I didn't hang up and neither did he.
I realized he didn't know how to.
It seemed he had put the phone in his shirt pocket
and forgot it there, like a bird he was showing
around, without any words, with only
the soft-handed cruelty of turning it towards the world.
I sat there listening to mostly silence
except for the sounds of his moving about,
a door closed, the refrigerator opened,
something picked up and kept back on the table,
the frame of time enough to have wondered about
anything from its weight
to the speed with which it had pierced his life
to land here.
It was a kind of quiet music that stretched
over minutes as he went about his day
which sounded alien and familiar in
queasy turns. A song that plays
in the overhead speakers at the supermarket
right as you pick up a perfectly good tangerine
and put it back down for no reason.
Soon the battery on her phone died.
I remember one of the last sounds, an almost sigh.
The kind belonging to a man alone

on the South Pole, who had misplaced something
that could be anywhere in the world.

"It seemed he had put the phone in his shirt pocket and forgot it there, like a bird he was showing around, without any words..."

— from "Quiet Music" by Abhishek Mehta

FLASH FICTION CONTEST FINALIST

LUCY ZHANG

GLASS WALL

THE FEW OF US who still work do so behind glass walls. It's for our safety. Before the establishment of the glass walls, cases of customers mauling employees due to "dissatisfaction" would spring up every other day. I had read studies on this: interpersonal human interaction had apparently become so rare that the rare encounter could trigger suppressed aggression. The rationale had to do with the hypothalamus's repressive ability when chatting back-and-forth with a bot versus screaming and strangling a person—I didn't fully understand mechanics or neurosurgical jargon.

We're safe now, though. Safely behind aluminosilicate glass that even the most determined and equipped of customers can't break, though the wall has accumulated plenty of fist prints and blood stains. I find it a little awkward trying to connect with customers from behind a layer of glass, but I suppose my actual work suffers no impediment. My clients and I can still speak from the microphones. The whole job is verbal, at the end of the day.

"How are you feeling?"

"It seems like you have some deeply held resentment despite your apparent forgiveness ..."

"Do you consider yourself living, surviving, or coping?"

Things like that. Things AI can say easily too, but there are a handful of people out there who need humans to speak to, and so my line of work remains useful. I am grateful, else I'd have to earn money cleaning baseboards or picking stone fruits under the unforgiving sun—the few things that escaped automation and remain tolerable enough for people like us who once studied to be cardiac surgeons and systems engineers and acquisition lawyers.

This line of work makes enough money for me to comfortably afford a nice plate of roast scallops and cordyceps hen soup once a month, an apartment in one of the complexes where windows open to a few trees before the view meets more concrete, and weekly payments to the kid I send to my parents so they have someone to complain about their migraines to since the AI is "too polite." I've told them many times that they can adjust the setting and make it meaner, but they refuse. They say it isn't natural. The kid I hired behaves nicely, even though his entire friend base, teachers, parents, and coaches are AI. He's the textbook perfect child that my parents would've drooled over whenever my teen self would emerge from my room after 7 a.m. on a weekend. My parents insisted that good kids participate in family activities—really, they just wanted an extra pair of hands to knead dough for scallion buns, even though they possessed a perfectly functional bread maker to do that.

"Have you ever participated in 'family activities'?" I once asked the kid.

"I talk to my family all the time," was his reply. His AI family, sure.

Kids these days all have AI families. Some of my clients mention it to me as a reason why they believe they've raised their children the best way. You give your kid an AI sister, AI brother, AI mom, AI dad, maybe even an AI dog. The full set is quite expensive but touted to raise children with unparalleled love, care, and extensive expertise that a single human could never replicate.

"What do *you* like to do with your child?" I like to ask these clients.

"Raise them." "Feed them." "I conceived them." The typical responses.

"That's not something you do with them," I would like to say. But I know not to say this. I did it once before the glass wall got erected, and the mother reached over and tried to rip off my ear while screaming that I couldn't listen properly. The mother wore a set of jagged diamond rings that scraped me from cheekbone to chin while she latched onto my ear like a snapping turtle.

"You're doing everything you can, so you shouldn't blame yourself," I instead say. "It's the AI that's not optimal for your family." And then I hand them a list of more expensive alternatives I've never personally vetted. If a client can afford human therapists, they can afford a more expensive AI. The list must help somewhat, since the same parents come back for their next session like they've found the meaning to life, and their newest, most urgent problem is now how their own AI only recommends healthy recipes. I like these problems the most. Not the children-raising ones. The undesirable-AI-response ones.

"It's making a recommendation with your wellness in its heart, but it's not contemplating your happiness," I say and nod sagely. "Your happiness comes with no price tag, but your lifespan is something more measurable. An entity so nearsighted can only give you such limited advice. But you've got a good head, and plenty of wise judgment. The first step is coming to us for help."

Recently, I've even started knocking softly on the glass to remind them I'm physically there as a source of comfort. Clients can forget they're looking at a human when glass hides our body heat and microphones conceal the tremor of our voices.

After work, I stop by my parents' place to make sure they're still alive. A recent study indicated that those without deep AI integration are more prone to suicide, but I think that one is a hoax. Or at least, the researchers' sample size was too small, and they've never seen people like my parents, debating the freshness of a salmon fish head while chopping ginger and scallions, sneaking bites of fried sesame balls before dinner while they think the other isn't watching, calling for me to bring a fresh jar of Lao Gan Ma because they know I like my meals a tad spicier. ◆

ABIGAIL CLOUD

THE FATHER,

timber-framed, says the poems need
to be dug up like grown potatoes, the dirt
scrubbed off. Speaking of the farm: Remember
the cows, the corn planter. The board feet
of walnut at rest. Nuts drop to the lawn,
meats kerneled tight. We find them empty
in barn dust, half-skull shells dropped
from the rafters. Beside them, more skulls,
forelegs, haunches dragged in to feed
foxes, kits snugged into the Model A's
shredded seats. Remember the old
radiator, the crosscut saw blades, the scythe,
all of that. Poems and walnuts pressed
into the dirt. Potatoes, potatoes, potatoes.

FLASH FICTION CONTEST FINALIST

COLLEEN BARAN

SHE HAS A NEW JOB COLLECTING DUES

AT FIRST, she's collecting membership dues, but soon she's collecting lists of due dates for upcoming births, and then when there aren't enough babies, she's collecting library book due dates and then just lists she finds on the ground of overdue tasks, but she actually only finds one of those—so it's onto lists of when the buses are due and what their lateness is due to, like bad tires and bad tempers and bad temperatures that melt the tires, and the tired bus driver who wishes he could retire. At the end of the week, she reports all her lists, and the computer gives her credits for food that she doesn't even have to stand in line for, and she uses the best-before dates that she finds on cans for her next list of dues, and the computer accepts them without even reading them. So she branches off into lists of what times people are due to arrive at work, and then lists of what they think their problems are due to, and she nearly pays a whole month's rent, just listing her best friend's problems with her mom, she's so lucky, and so she pretends to be a therapist, even though that's a job only computers have these days. And she does try to pretend to be a computer, but no one believes that she's realistic enough at the job. So she gets bad reviews as too stilted, too awkward, ill-informed, and not sympathetic enough, which she spends hours talking about with her own computer therapist and which she can list as due to her own human fallibility, after the computer explains it to her, in soothing tones, in soft tones, in tones as soft as the soft spot on a newborn baby's head, which reminds her that she needs to get to work, so she goes to the hospital and finds due dates for two new babies and then goes down to the morgue and finds people who've died—due to cancer and suicide and heart attacks—and she's so happy to have found something she's good at. She could do this job all day. Due to reasons the computer explains to her that night, after she gets home from work, she listens to its voice, giving her the recognition she knows she's due. ◆

YAN ZHANG

小作文[1]

The sky glowed azure
above the field, still morning-wet. Daisies
rang along the sidewalk. Yellow petals guarded

pedestrians' hearts, curling in the 留下[2]'s wind.
I took a picture so the future could prove the light
once fell like this. Exactly this way, each pixel

piecing together precise shards of what we remember:
the swollen sky, the clouds billowing & blood-
shot orange, not cliché until I said *let's go*
to Shanghai & you laughed. *I'm like*

a dog & you're the mother.
                                        Why not   reach for a city to name
the nameless drift between us. You knew it

before I did—so I said 光阴似箭, 日月如梭.
What's so cliché about that? Waiting to resurface
months later, the answer unspools

through my phone's camera roll as I scroll
through memories: its loftiness, your breath's
little note between 箭 [arrow] & 梭 [shuttle], knowing

the punchline would soon scatter into shadows
across the pavement. Maybe it was the way
we wrote it—overwrote it—through elementary school

[小作文] until the last Chinese cicada shuttered.

In the background of those memories, the bench
still glows with the question you asked, how
to translate 光阴 [time] without sacrificing the swiftness & swagger

of departure. It's still morning-wet, the daisies still
ringing the meaning's *light & shade* along the sidewalk:
日's [day's] sun, 月's [month's] moon.

But *time flew by like an arrow. Days slipped*
through like a weaver's shuttle. The translation
faded into the wrong light—into pixels, blurred by time.

1 *xiǎo zuò wén,* the direct translation is "little essay."
2 *liúxià,* name of the street, the direct translation is "stay."

FLASH FICTION CONTEST FINALIST

DOMINIC VITI

TRADERS

LAST MONTH every house on our street had a yard sale. Nobody coordinated the event. It was one of those what-are-the-chances type of deals.

We all got up bright and early to unload our things on the grass and driveway, watching the people next door unload things on their grass and driveway, who watched the people next door to them do the same thing. Then we all sat there in lawn chairs, pretending not to look at each other. It is shameful enough putting a bunch of garbage in front of your house and asking people to pay for it. But for all of us to do it together, we did not look good as a group.

It confirmed our desperation, that we all needed money. It confirmed our recklessness, that we wasted what money we had on shit we didn't need.

And it was shit. All of it: burnt frying pans, old stereo equipment, rollerblades missing wheels. We presented our unwanteds in an orderly fashion on tables or in cases like it was in a store—a store that had cardboard boxes arranged on bedsheets spread across the lawn, sheets on which we conceived our children and now used to sell their toys.

After a while, out of guilt or boredom, we left our chairs to go house to house. There is only so much time you can give the average person before they have to buy something.

Then the strangest thing happened. Instead of buying, we started trading. People were swapping left and right, exchanging the items we would have thrown out if we did not make a sale for items we would have bought in an actual store, for more, had we actually sold them. By the end of the afternoon, everyone on our street had traded everything they had.

But before we could take our new things back in the house, cars began pulling up to the curb and families from all over town, who had followed the many yard sale signs on street corners, started shopping. Nobody said no. The money begged.

Instead of keeping the new things we needed, we watched from our garages as strangers bartered for our memories that our neighbors sold for cheap. We watched them sell our birthday gifts, our keepsakes and prized possessions. It was like they were stealing from us. Stealing parts of us. That was how we looked at it, at each other. Traitors.

After that we all stopped talking to each other. There have been no more cookouts, no block parties. It used to be if someone was sick, a neighbor would bring over soup or bake a casserole. Now we avoid eye contact at the mailbox. In one month, more than half the people on our street have put their house on the market. This has only deepened our contention.

Every yard with a For Sale sign. ◆

ELIZABETH ROSE BRUCE

DEAR DYLAN

If I had known back then,
just teenagers hooking up
in your little blue Pontiac Firebird
outside of that trailer park
party, accidentally honking the horn
with my ass, beckoning
the partygoers to the trailer's porch,
where they whooped
and wooed and pointed at
our pale tangled limbs spilling
out of that messy car,
as we stretched tight clothes
back over our bodies in that bright
December spotlight,

if I had known you would die
only a few years later
at the house you grew up in —
I remember your bus stop
— would become addict, dead
at 24, a phone call from my brother
who saw it on Facebook,
a poem I write years later —
I would have stayed
in the car, young and drunk on
shotgunned Millers, long after
the bonfire burned out,
laughed along with the watchers
as I kissed your
cold face a little longer.

FLASH FICTION CONTEST FINALIST

RODRIGO SCHÖNARDIE

TAKE ME THERE

I PARK THE RENTED CAR on the side of the dirt track. The four plane trees confirm I am at the right place. I step out, close the door without locking it, look around and breathe in the fresh air. It smells of earth and undergrowth. The plane leaves rustle with the breeze and, if I make an effort, I can hear the sound of the stream coming from within the woods, on the other side of the track. Apart from the plane trees, there is no trace left of the home where my grandparents and their offspring once lived: four daughters, like the trees, and one son. I search further ahead for the ruins of the old butcher's, and I find them, covered by vegetation that conceals the remnants, as if protecting them from the passage of time that has taken nearly everything already.

We used to visit this land, deep in the countryside, from my childhood until early adulthood. Then I left my hometown to live abroad, far away, in another country. Just as my mother, uncles, and grandparents had left that place to live in the nearby town, before I was born. I don't remember ever going there by public transport; none reached it anymore by the time I was a child. Years before, it was my grandfather who was in charge of the buses that connected the area to town, and before him, his father, with ox carts. My grandfather was a businessman, the owner of the buses that ran the route to the city, the dance hall, the butcher's beside the house, the football field at the back, and the plot where, on the other side of the house, the school was built.

From my early memories of these visits, I remember the school, modest and small, still standing but then inactive; I also remember an old-style school desk, left outside, that maybe my father, my mother or another relative had once used. The school and the house, both made of wood, were knocked down. The plane trees remained. We used to jump over the barbed wire fence, already rusty and no longer keeping much out, to sit under their shade, to make a barbecue on an improvised grill and drink *chimarrão*. Parents, uncles, aunts, and cousins gathered together again, my grandparents no longer with us, telling or listening to stories of the time they had lived there. There were still a few acquaintances scattered around, and each time we would pay them a visit, stopping from house to house.

I enjoyed imagining life in that place, at the time my family lived there. The dance hall and its dances, the football matches on the field where my father used to play and where he met my mother; I imagined the classes and the punishments I had heard about, like kneeling on corn kernels. All that was left was one or two walls of the old butcher's, the only one made of brick. The neighbors, who were never many, became fewer and fewer, having passed away or being forced to move to town.

Once, I tried to buy the plot that belonged to my grandfather, when it was still affordable. I wanted to build a cottage, have some time close to nature and my roots, and create new memories. They didn't want to sell it. Fools. The land is there, abandoned. The whole place, abandoned.

My mother, the youngest of the daughters, died first; then the oldest, the second daughter and, most recently, my uncle. There is one aunt left.

And the plane trees. The barbecues and picnics no longer happen, but the trees are still standing, waiting for me to come back. That's what I want to believe.

The place exists. My trip with a rented car, only in my imagination. I don't even drive. What I know is what is told to me; almost no one lives there anymore, no one visits, the place has become a no-man's land, and it has even become dangerous. But I am sure that, if I go, I will recognize the spot, because the plane trees will be there, grandiose, in front of where the house once stood. One day I will return, and I will sit under their shade, protected by their branches, *chimarrão* in hand. I will spend an afternoon, or even a whole day, and the plane trees will tell me stories of my family. ◆

FLASH FICTION CONTEST FINALIST

ABBY MANZELLA

THE BOOKKEEPERS

ONE DAY, not that long ago, the libraries closed. It happened gradually with signs on websites and doors appearing day after day—spread from county to county like the disease that caused the closures. "For the foreseeable future ..." the signs read, but we could not foresee what such a future would hold without the bags of books for reading groups, the children's storytimes, the cozy nooks that each of us held dear, the access to research issues big and small in our lives, and so much more that happened in those grand public spaces.

Then the book industry fell without the library purchases as support, and the printing presses ceased: a technology with thousands of years of history from the first printed texts in China to wood and metal block lettering, from Wang Cheng's mass-produced book to Guttenberg's press, was quietly stilled in the end, and pigmented oils no longer stamped a single page. We felt the hole where an undiminished good had once rested.

Not that all the books were gone, of course. This was no *Fahrenheit 451* of book bonfires, not because of a drastic shift in social reasoning but for fear that the volumes' contaminants would spread even wider. See, our society spurned the sharing of written language after the latest disease was found to proliferate via paper. It inoculated book pages with ease and the next reader along with it. The published word passed along a deadly knowledge like the fictional fatalities once caused by licking the poisoned pages of Aristotle's lost *Treatise on Comedies.* In our world, though, it was a natural virus that required only a fingertip to a story's surface to yield the lethal consequences. The contagion jumped from paper to hand to nose to throat, and readers started to fall.

We didn't want to talk about the virus, though, or the friends it struck down quickly—like lightning but not as rare—so we focused on perfume. You could buy these new scents for a song, replicating "that new-book smell," and even "that old-volume-from-your-grandmother scent." The air was soon filled with familiar notes of ink and adhesives along with the lingering fragrance of dust and mold, reminiscent of, but not quite, the thing itself.

Other commercial products soon emerged, most notably the one-handed stress reducers that let your fingers imitate the pattern of the turning of a page. Over and over, without a word read, it functioned to reduce anxiety. *Are you a right hand top or a left hand cross-over-the-page-at-the-bottom turner?* Neighbors would ask these questions with palpable nostalgia from the safety of their front porches. Turners, as the gadgets were called, were all the rage during online meetings that extended beyond their pre-set times—as they all did. In our own homes we stayed safe and untouched.

After the libraries closed, those who bemoaned the loss whispered about the copies they possessed. Alone in their homes, drinking Amontillado in newly converted basement libraries, readers caressed the books they had. Dog-earing became criminal in the minds of many, if it wasn't already, but no one would ever know the culprits, since neighbors no longer saw each other's books.

Eventually personal libraries became valorized over previously posh spaces like wine cellars or screening rooms. Hardbacks and paperbacks were consigned to well-lit locations and organizational patterns, posted on social media, showing the owner's dedication to words from the old-fashioned color-coded order to the structure based on the book's age with the oldest—the most venerated—in the top left corner. Some did it for the artistic effect, but many continued to read with a fervor.

Still, other people didn't much notice the change of the status of tattered bindings, having not been to a library since their school days. *Why all the hubbub?* they asked. *Life goes on. There are other pastimes, like sports.* And it was true that outdoor sports held less of a risk, with pliant masks now common and professional players taking the risk that remained for a necessary paycheck. And it was true that the animal hides on balls seemed not to retain the disease like the pulp of trees. So some leaned easily into their recliners to receive their digital entertainment and their sole access to information.

Time wore on, and the books sat beloved, or ignored, and we all kept our hands to ourselves, or most did. We now knew that the words would fade, the pages would crumble, and the spines, once strong, would go slack. Some thought that online research could replace that dusty old knowledge that had been amassed over centuries, but artificial intelligence was the access point to all data now, and it directed and synthesized as it would with a confidence that few disputed. Conspiracy theories flourished in headlines, and few read beyond the technologically created highlights to check even the online sources referenced, which themselves were all digitally malleable with the push of a button. Those in power could change or delete "facts" at will.

As the days turned to months, turned to years—like the pages of a story—we realized that life would never turn back to what it had been. This was a new world, but perhaps one we should have seen coming. We held close what was cherished and lived on. If we had books, they remained tucked away and not shared, and each of us, buoyed by our own concerns and reasons, only shouted to each other from afar. ◆

WENDY WISNER

MY MOTHER'S BODY

The doctor says I should be grateful for my mother's
healthy body, which houses a brain that can no longer
read a book or remember how to make a piece of toast.
Even as her legs shuffle across the floor, her body roots her
in place, an oak tree. Her hair a mess of flaming red leaves.
Skin a shiny brown paper bag. I touch it as I fall asleep.
She could live in this body forever, while her mind
runs laps on the wet, muddy soccer field. My mother
reaches for her mind as she rifles through her purse
searching for her phone. *I'm sure it's in here*, she says.
She places a Styrofoam cup on the chair in the doctor's
waiting room, knocks it over with her elbow.
Her elbows are macaroni. They glisten like wet leaves.
I watch the cup fall to the floor in slow motion.

"She could live in this body forever, while her mind runs laps on the wet, muddy soccer field."

— from "My Mother's Body" by Wendy Wisner

FLASH FICTION CONTEST FINALIST

ASHLEY W. CUNDIFF

THE RULES OF JIM'S POND

THESE ARE THE RULES of Jim's pond: Don't litter. If you catch the white catfish or the silver grass carp, throw it back. If you catch anything, throw it back, unless you're hungry.

Uncle Jim's dead now, but the rules still apply. The pond keeps track. I know this because I know the pond the best. Been fishing there every day since I was sixteen months old, and now I'm sixteen years old. These days I fish at Jim's pond more than anyone, heading over as soon as school's out and staying until dusk every day from the first chirp of the spring peepers until ice shards circle the water's edge. And I know things like this: There's an old Ford pickup submerged way deep on the far side, which is where you want to sink your line if you're looking for something big. The Ford's cab is teeming with old catfish, filling its crevices with their dark, oily bodies. In its bed are forty empty quart-size jars that Gus Lee used to use to carry his best corn liquor.

Gus considered himself Jim's best friend and so entitled to stopping by the pond to throw in a line on his way home from his route every Saturday morning, the empty jars he'd traded back for full ones rattling behind him. But one particular Saturday morning, Pierce Pelham, the town's oldest deputy, was rattling behind him too, so Gus decided to dump the truck in the pond, on account of it needed a new suspension, anyway. But somehow Gus got his foot tangled in the seat belt he never wore, and the Ford dragged him straight through the young poplars crowding the steep bank and pinned him underwater. It took the Ford a day or two to sink into the muck and disappear. It took Gus less than three minutes to drown in six feet of depth. That's the way Jim told it to me, anyway. There's no littering at Jim's pond.

Uncle Jim died six months ago, like this: Shortly after having his breakfast biscuit, he tossed in a line and caught a small bluegill. The bluegill caught the attention of a brown water snake, which clamped its jaws around it and did not let go as Jim reeled them both in. Jim stared that son of a bitch straight in the eye until it released its jaws, dropped to the ground, and struck him on the right calf muscle before slithering like crazy into the woods. The fish was already wrecked, no use throwing him back. The pond can tell a dead fish from a live one. And the snake was long gone, no tossing his ass back in, either. Jim went in his house, stuck a Band-Aid on his leg, made sure his bills were paid up, called up Patty Bridges to confess that he'd loved her his whole life, and cracked open a beer. The infection set in fast and strong; the leg was black in two days and Jim was gone in a week. Even he had to follow the rules.

The pond had never belonged to anyone but Jim, who had dug the hole and dammed the spring himself, but my dad thought it'd be better in the form of liquid cash. He tried to sell Jim's little house and the pond along with it to Miles Burdich, the town's most popular auctioneer. The deal didn't go through; Miles thought to throw in a line while taking a look at the property. With more luck than skill he caught the white catfish, its skin a match for the white leather seats in his Mercedes, and quick as he could he slit its belly and drove it to the nearest convenience store to be weighed for a trophy citation.

Miles wasn't paying much attention to his surroundings as he struggled across the parking lot with the bloody fish slung over his shoulder. This was unfortunate, as it happened that just then Mabel Pritchett pulled up in her boat of a Lumina, stopping to pick up a tomato for her lunch sandwich after a routine eye exam. The sudden emergence of the sun from behind a cloud overwhelmed Mabel's eyes, sensitive from dilation drops, and flustered, she mistook the brake for the gas and barreled right over Miles and the fish. You can't just leave the premises and expect the pond rules not to apply.

My dad passed away a week later—a brain aneurysm. I found him in Jim's kitchen, phone in hand—he'd been taking pictures of the pond and house for a property listing. The photos of the house were good enough, as good as you could get of a house like Jim's—pretty much a single-wide with a solid foundation. The photos of the pond were strange, though—the clear water, always bottle green in real life, appeared a flat tan, and the trees had no leaves even though it was the middle of June.

These are the rules of Jim's pond: Don't litter. If you catch the white catfish or the silver grass carp, throw it back. If you catch anything, throw it back, unless you're hungry. The pond is not for sale.

They buried my dad in the Methodist churchyard, but I scattered my uncle's ashes in the pond. Catfish swam up in droves, thinking I was tossing in breadcrumbs, and the silver grass carp came too, making ripples across the water before it surfaced feet from the edge. I didn't throw in a line that day, out of respect for Jim and the pond, but I was back the next afternoon with my rod. I caught six little bluegill and one big catfish and threw them all back. Jim always said you and the pond both would know it if you were hungry enough to keep one, and I've yet to experience that sort of pang. ◆

MATTHEW J. SPIRENG

AN OLD STORY

We were told the horses were coming,
so we waited. But days later, weakened
with hunger, we knew there would be

no horses, and we began killing. It
was not what some would have expected, but
we were desperate. Some wondered who

had lied about the horses. No one confessed,
and then, just as the killing seemed about to
subside, we heard the distant sound of horses.

Who, some wondered, had begun the killing,
who had first despaired? And some insisted
the killing continue even as the horses arrived.

"We were told the horses were coming..."

— from "An Old Story" by Matthew J. Spireng

MILLY HELLER

BESET

A YOUNG WOMAN, Caitlin, bought the house next door to us. Before she moved in, she got Mouton's Tree Service to cut down a banyan tree in her front yard that was one hundred years old and fifty-five inches in diameter. That united the neighbors, including me, against her. My husband said, "Let's wait before thinking badly of her." He had noticed things about the tree as he walked our dog. He said new leaves dropped off the moment they appeared, and a thin layer of fungus coated the trunk.

One morning, he got the first glimpse of Caitlin. She was meeting with her contractor. I asked him what she seemed like.

"Like she works out a lot," he said.

"How old is she?"

"Young. Early thirties?"

We were in our late fifties.

Caitlin moved in a month later. My husband talked to her in the mornings as they got into their cars. She was a medical researcher at Touro Infirmary. Oncology. My husband, Jim, told me I'd really like her. "She went to Mt. Carmel and LSU. She grew up in Metairie. All her life she's heard how uptown is full of crime, so she moved back to Metairie when she started at Touro. That's when she realized uptown is great and Metairie's boring. She said she's super excited to be here."

"She said that? Super excited?"

He said, "Stop."

"She cut down a banyan tree that was one hundred years old and fifty-five inches in diameter."

"She had three arborists come look at it. Each one told her it was dying. Each one told her it was about to fall on the house. Banyan trees can't take our winters. It's strange the tree lived so long. She said she sobbed her heart out when it came down."

"She said that? Sobbed her heart out?"

He said, "Don't."

FLEAS INFESTED our house. They moved in before Caitlin did, so I couldn't blame the invasion on her. The vet assured me our dog wasn't the source, because I gave him his flea pill every month. The exterminator said a nocturnal animal, probably an opossum, was sleeping all day under our house and until we got rid of it there was no point in spraying. Like most New Orleanians, we lived in a raised house. The grates blocking the openings beneath the house had rusted, and a few swung loose. I hired the neighborhood handyman to replace them. The opossum stayed away; the fleas stuck around.

The living room harbored the most fleas, with the kitchen a close second. Whenever a flea jumped on me, I pinched it in triumph and raced to drown it in a solution I'd mixed, as the internet instructed, of Blue Dawn and water. I spent hours standing in one place, staring at my legs and feet. I wore socks because the fleas got trapped in the fibers. White socks were best for attracting and spotting the fleas, but I pinched and plucked my white socks so much they all started to unravel.

Staring at my feet, I got to know the skin on my calves and ankles. I told myself the glimpses of light blue veins looked like delicate brush strokes. I told myself the purplish undertone was graceful and the scatter of flea bites subtle. I told myself not to wear shorts outside of the house.

ONE SATURDAY, when I was getting out of my car—I'd just come back from Sports Authority, where I bought more white socks—Caitlin stopped beside me, because my open car door was blocking her way. She wore chic black workout clothes and had been on a run. Her blond hair was so glossy and straight she could've stopped at a blow-dry bar on her run. Also, a teeth-whitening bar. Not to mention an I'm-a-much-warmer-person-than-I-look bar. I introduced myself to her. She paused whatever she was playing on her iPhone, though she kept the earbuds in her ears. We often called out "hello" to each other and exchanged comments on the heat as I checked for mail, watered the plumbago, and picked basil from the pots on our front porch, but this was our first time talking face-to-face.

She said, "Do you live around here?"

NOW THAT WE'D BATTENED DOWN the hatches, the exterminator agreed to spray. He said we had to leave the house for four hours after he sprayed. Jim said, "Let's make it a nice afternoon. Let's go to the Ogden and a bookstore, or coffee shop."

I said, "Southern art, no thank you."

He said, "How about NOMA?"

"We were there two weeks ago."

He didn't say anything.

I said, "Okay, the Ogden."

On the way to the Ogden, I folded my long flowered skirt above my knees so I could check my legs for fleas. The sky boiled hot blue above us despite a thunderstorm whirling in charcoal not too far ahead, above the Mississippi. Our phone alarms blew up, warning of floods.

I said, "What with the vermin, my prairie skirt, and the thunderstorm, it's like we're pioneers."

Jim said, "Please don't bring up the Oregon Trail. I'll have flashbacks." About fifteen years ago, when our daughters were in middle school, they became obsessed with the *Hardscrabble History* books. They told Jim, since he liked the history of the West, to read the one about the Oregon Trail. The girls had gone on their merry way after reading it, but Jim zombied around, murmuring, "The deaths, you wouldn't believe it. Two little girls foraged for vegetables but picked hemlock by mistake. The whole family died in convulsions, foaming at the mouth."

A flea sped down my calf. I nabbed it, rolled down the window, and tossed it.

I said, "We're about to hit our own Oregon Trail. The fleas are an omen."

"They are not an omen. If you were reading a novel where the family's house got fleas, and the fleas foreshadowed the family's downfall, you would hate it. You'd say the symbolism was over-obvious."

"I'd be wrong."

CAITLIN KNOCKED on the door late one afternoon while I was standing in the hallway checking my legs. Since the exterminator's visit I had seen only a few fleas. For the amount of time I still stood around examining my legs, the ratio of fleas to hours should have been higher.

"Please come in." I was conscious of my ratty T-shirt, old gym shorts, and bright white socks.

Caitlin said, "Oh my God, I love your house."

"With the girls grown up and gone, it's too much house for us."

"*Too much house.* What a terrific expression. I love that you said that."

"You do?" But I was flattered. I worked for twenty years as a claims adjuster, and writing up reports was my favorite part of the job. One of my coworkers, Kevin, and I wrote reports for each other in different genres. My favorites were gothic, rich with *sepulchral miasmas, muttering reverberations,* and *bosky, beckoning doomscapes.* But when the hurricanes hitting New Orleans grew more colossal and catastrophic, Kevin became distraught at the damage we surveyed and moved with his boyfriend to Cincinnati. A few years later the agency pulled out of Louisiana, saying it couldn't afford the payouts. I retired to help take care of my parents, who were flailing, with valor and dignity, at a conspiracy of fatal diseases.

"*Too much house* is my problem. Well, one of my problems."

Caitlin had problems? I was beginning to like her.

Caitlin said, "The NIH, that's the National Institute—"

"Of Health, yes, I know."

"I should have known *you* would know."

The miasma of flattery was thick but helped make up for her model-like height, deep scientific knowledge of cancer cells, and *Do you live around here.* She said the NIH, because of budget cuts, canceled the grant funding her research at Touro. Caitlin was out of a job. "I thought cancer research was safe, right?"

"Right."

"To make my house note, I'm getting creative. My first project: an Airbnb. I've got the perfect set-up. My guests will use the side entrance."

That was the side closest to our house, with a strip of gravel between the two houses. She saw me glance toward it.

"I'd carefully screen my applicants."

"Parking is awfully tight on our street."

"I hope that won't keep anyone away."

"I mean parking is tight for those of us who live here."

"My listing stresses how close I am to the streetcar line. If you like I'll add there is no need to rent a car."

"Your *tenants* might drive here."

"My *guests* will figure out any parking problem." Her smile shifted from friendly to authoritative. She loomed vital, golden, dazzling; I felt scrawny, depleted. Often what I thought was a flea running along one of my legs turned out to be a strand of hair falling from my head to the floor. Caitlin held out the clipboard.

I let her keep the clipboard. "I'll talk it over with Jim."

"Jim didn't tell you? I mentioned it to him when he was walking Stanley. He said he was all for it."

"He did?" Mr. Nice Guy. People-Pleaser. Diplomat. Peace-at-any-Price.

She said, "Jim is a sweetheart," and I inserted *sweetheart* between *people-pleaser* and *diplomat* but as always, like in a black and white movie, a scroll unfurled listing his sterling qualities, and typewriter keys clicked as *fair-minded, witty, reads Jane Austen* outpaced the epithets.

"Speaking of sweethearts, your dog! I love Stanley. When Touro finds new funding, fingers crossed, my first stop is Zeus's Place to adopt a rescue, like you all did." She chatted away about her childhood dogs. She stood in a glare of light shooting in from the window. The sun was in her eyes, but I felt no pity; she'd slain the banyan tree that shaded our hallway. The glare was so acute, I spotted a flea hopping along one of her fancy white leather sneakers. The fleas I'd seen since the spraying were extra-small, slow, almost too easy to catch. Caitlin's was plump, and shiny as a beetle. It could star in a made-for-TV movie of Donne's poem, "The Flea" as the flea in which the two lovers' blood "mingled be." I needed patience. If I swooped now, the flea would sense my hand, jump to the dark hardwood floor, and be lost to me forever. Telepathically I urged it onto Caitlin's light gray sock; it leapt and landed precisely where I directed it, on the sock's plush, jaunty rim. My fingers flexed.

WHEN JIM GOT HOME from work, I was in the kitchen, peeling cucumbers for a salad. He said, "I just talked to Caitlin. It's like she was waiting for me. She showed me bruises on her knee and elbow. She said things here got weird today."

"I guess, but she didn't have to ambush you."

"She didn't ambush me."

"Would you rather miso-sesame dressing or the usual vinaigrette?"

"Whichever's easier to make. What happened with Caitlin?"

"She came over to talk about her Airbnb, and I saw a flea on her sock. I didn't want her to know we have fleas, gross, and I didn't want them to infiltrate *her* house, so I knelt down to get it." I hadn't knelt. Because the flea was disappearing into the fabric, I hit the floor. I slipped my finger between her skin and sock to work the flea out to where my left hand waited. The flea, still enmeshed, lowered itself to the body of the sock. Luckily, I knew that tactic. I braced my thumb against her ankle and dug toward the arch of her foot. Caitlin said, "What the hell?"

I said, "A bug got into your sock."

She reached down to swat it. I grabbed her wrist. She easily shook me off. I gripped her ankle with both of my hands and yanked her foot toward me. That's when she toppled.

To Jim I said, "The flea was in her sock. I tried to get it out, pulled on her sock maybe too hard, and she tripped over me. Good thing she didn't hit my bad shoulder."

He said, with entreaty, "You need to talk to someone." I added *concerned* to his good attributes, along with *boyishly handsome.*

I said, "I'll think about it," or something like that. What I wanted: Jim to leave the kitchen, before he noticed I harbored two fleas on my left sock and one on my right.

He said, "Remember, we're lined up for a second spraying. That will finish the fleas off for good."

"Excellent," I said thinking, *leave, leave, leave.* My goal was to accumulate five fleas, because that's how many frail fleas would make up for the robust specimen who'd left with Caitlin. Fleas are attracted to motion. To entice the last two, I'd been parading at regular intervals around the kitchen and living room while listening to show tunes.

"We'll get back to where we were," he said.

"That'll be nice."

"Pre-fleas," he said. "The golden age."

"I can't wait." Swiftly, furtively, I lifted my feet up and down, in case any guests on the floor wanted to hop aboard. ◆

LUCAS CARDONA

FROWNY FACE

I come home from work, crack a beer.
It's been a week, a year.
Suddenly, I forget to eat, forget
I'm a bad habit I can't break,
a thing that needs feeding, needs love
now more than ever.
Every night, the same old tears.
I'm not mocking Armageddon anymore.
I've grown cautious of what I disregard.
This piecemeal existence is fraught
with leftovers. Ditto this hip pouch of hope
I'll be a husband one day.
I've heard that silence breeds tenacity
but I just want someone to dance with
on the weekends and canoodle before bed.
When rejection becomes us
masturbation's just an SOS.
Nostalgia is killing me—they'll bury me in it.
Sometimes, I wish I lived in a century
when people still believed ghost stories
had meaning. We tell stories
when we're trying to be honest.
I keep telling myself the same one—
it's over; she's coming over!
All those nights I begged her to stay,
made her tea, massaged her neck and shoulders
until my hands went dumb.
Look, it's getting late. I know you're hungry.
We could share an apple or a pear.
We could eat a bunch of shit.
Drink all the wine. Sleep in.

I'll let you read my fortune
if you let me comb your hair.
Forever's just a bee buzzing in your ear—
nobody hears. Stop fretting
about tomorrow. I'm not waking up.
She's not even here.

BEN REED

MY TURN WITH THE WAND

WHEN IT WAS MY TURN with the wand, I got straight to work. I drove to my mother's house and passed the wand over her reclining body. A moment later she was up and out of her La-Z-Boy, walking around the carpeted den like the accident never happened.

Well? I asked. What do you think?

She was making little cuts and charges across the brown and orange shag, like a little kid trying out new sneakers.

My knees work! she said. It's a miracle!

It's actually magic, I explained.

On my way out she asked if I might also do something about the house—the paint, the rotted fascia, the loose bricks in the chimney. I waved the wand at her leaning split-level and in two shakes it was the nicest house in town. A three-story Victorian with bay windows and fish-scale shingling inside gothic gables, everything made from that old redwood you can't find anymore, because all those trees are gone.

I drove to the sad side of town and let myself into my dad's apartment. He was smoking a Doral 100, sitting in his own La-Z-Boy, the other half of the pair of recliners separated in the divorce. He was watching the Padres on TV. I waved the wand over his body and he sprang up, too.

He cried out, Hey! I feel great!

I fixed your rheumatism, I said. And your gout, your edema, your nicotine addiction, your chronic fatigue.

But my eyes! he said, stubbing out his cigarette. I can't even see the TV!

I said, Take off your glasses.

He did and said, Oh my God.

Nope, I said. Just magic.

Later I was stopped at a red light at the bottom of a highway off-ramp, right next to a family of panhandlers. They were huddled on a narrow sliver of concrete by the overpass, the father holding the usual cardboard sign: Anything Helps, etc. His sunburnt wife and his gangly teenage son were on the ground behind him, looking downtrodden and glum. I put my car's top down and waved the wand at them. Instantly the father stood up straight, healthy and clean. His son was now as sturdy and hale as a teenager ought to be, his clothing mended and pressed. The mother, suddenly beautiful, sat on the ground staring at her hands and prodding her legs in disbelief. For a second I was distracted. The magic had done something with her hair.

Sir, what is the meaning of this? the father demanded. He sounded scared for some reason.

I fixed you up, I said, trying not to seem defensive. Now you can have good lives. Normal lives.

We're still poor, though, the kid said. Although he did not say this in a disrespectful way.

I waved the wand again. I said, Not anymore.

The kid's mom was holding a Prada shoulder bag. She pulled out fistfuls of cash and credit cards. She found a ring with two keys—one for a mansion in the hills west of town, another for the Range Rover parked in the driveway.

The father started to say something else, but I couldn't hear him. The light had changed and somebody behind me had honked. Then somebody else honked. Then it sounded like everyone in the world was honking, like everyone in the world had been waiting forever to turn left, and I was blocking the only green arrow.

THERE WERE RULES, of course. The main one being that the magic in the wand is finite—or rather, finite per user. It runs out on you eventually. The second rule is that bigger feats use more magic, so you can't go all over the world fixing everyone's problems until utopia. You can't just *cure* cancer or end the suffering of children. You can't wave the wand at the UN and say, Peace in the Middle East. If you tried to do a huge thing like that you'd fail and burn through all of your allotted magic without accomplishing jack. So you set your sights on smaller things. If you can't restore your parents' marriage, you heal their broken bodies. You can't end poverty, so you do a little guerilla philanthropy, like fixing up some panhandlers you meet at an intersection. Inzephaar, a wizard who'd had the wand a dozen turns before me, wrote online that one can expect seventy or eighty regular-sized feats before the wand is spent and needs to be abandoned. That was the final rule: When the wand has been used up, you have to lose it. You can't keep it, it won't recharge, you can't pass it on. You have to throw it in the bushes from a speeding train or drop it in a river. The wand must be lost and change possession before it will work again. It has to be discovered anew.

I DROVE to the gym and cancelled my membership. (I'd already given myself the body you see before you.) As I left, I waved the wand at all of the overweight people sweating away on the stationary bikes and treadmills, and again at all the scrawny and sketchy-looking people in the weightlifting area. In a flash, all of the overweight people were svelte and trim, and all the scrawny and sketchy-looking people doing squats and bench-presses and whatnot were totally jacked, with bulging neck muscles and six-packs and veins rippling their arms. There was general confusion, and a lot of suddenly too-tight or too-loose Lycra, but mostly people were excited.

After the gym thing I was feeling superficial. To get myself grounded again, I made it so that all the dogs in the animal shelter—and all the cats, and iguanas, and cockatiels, and the lone boa constrictor on his artificial branch—were adopted by kind people who would give them loving homes. I didn't even have to go in the animal shelter. I did that one in my car, from the parking lot. I was about to drive away when my father called. He said now that he can walk again, he wants to make the Grand Tour. See Athens, Paris, Rome. I said I'd make it happen.

IT WAS NIGHTTIME when I magicked my way into the convalescent home to see Mr. Martens, my favorite teacher in high school. He taught English, but really what he taught us was irony and iambic pentameter and vicariousness, and about the potent and transitive properties of symbolism and metaphor. He instructed us as seriously as if we were being initiated into a cult. Come to think of it, he was a lot of people's favorite teacher. We used to drive by his house on the weekend and catch him in his garden, pulling up weeds and carrots. Years later, while riding his bicycle to school, Mr. Martens hit a pothole and fell in the road and was hit by a delivery van. He survived, but with a permanent impairment. He couldn't remember names or faces or track the days from one to the next. He could still recite "To His Coy Mistress," but he would forget to eat, and he'd wake up and think he was back at Oxford. Obviously, he couldn't teach. The hospitalization and treatments bankrupted his family. His wife had a breakdown trying to care for him while maintaining her own career. His children grew up and scattered like leaves. Mr. Martens washed ashore at Comfort Cove Nursing Home, where he has been ever since. I heard he had not spoken in two years.

I waved the wand over his sleeping body, and he sat up instantly. He knew exactly who I was.

I said, How do you feel?

Mr. Martens said, Before the accident my greatest fear was that I was going to hell—not for my mistakes, necessarily, but for my cowardice. For all the times I let beauty depart my doorway because I was too fearful to answer the call. I could have been a professor. I could have been poet laureate. But what I love most of all is a static situation. My preference is to remain at rest. Like the Underground Man I luxuriate in my inertia. Eventually it got into my head that my particular hell would simply be this life without change, stuck on repeat, unending. Too late did I yearn for change. The day I tried to fix my life was the day I got run over by the bread truck. As I lay there, I thought: *Justice.* But later I realized that my cognitive enfeeblement—while tragic for my loved ones, certainly, and inconvenient to me personally, of that there can be no doubt—was a fortuitous circumvention of the thing I dreaded most: infinite recursion, normality without variation. Sweet Jesus, I lost my memory! Blessed unconsciousness, bring me to thy bosom!

I crossed my arms and said, Well that's a fine thank-you.

Because of you, Mr. Martens said, the galling prospect of such a dreadful fate has found me again, like an unstoppable curse, like some terrible jinx.

I showed him the wand. It's just magic, I said.

I left in a sour mood. You're not supposed to get mad at people for telling you the truth, but I couldn't help it. I thought about changing Mr. Martens's attitude, just a smidgen, although by now I was worried about the wand running low. Also, using magic to change someone's mind felt artless, like cheating. Like a violation. So instead, I waved the wand in the air to patch every pothole in town, fill every crack, and smooth every sidewalk buckled by roots.

I drove down Park Street, inspecting the new roads from my convertible. I saw a guy who had a deformed face and a hunchback and one of those shrunken, misshapen arms. I waved the wand at him without stopping. In the rearview I saw him, stunned and blinking at the reflection of his perfect body in the display window of the toy store. I honked just to say, That was me! but I didn't stop. I did that one as a drive-by, after the heavy trip Mr. Martens had laid on me.

On Broadway, a car in front of me was really moving. I thought, At least somebody is out here enjoying the smooth new roads. A dog darted into the road, and the speeding car ran over its back legs. The other driver and I stopped and got out. The poor creature was small, a spaniel, practically still a puppy, wailing in pain as it kept trying to stand on the fresh asphalt. The other driver turned away, weeping with her face in her hands.

A boy no older than ten came running up to me, sobbing. It was his dog, and he recognized me as the guy with the wand. (By then, everybody in town knew about me.) He pulled on my coat, begging me to save his dog, Daisy. I said, Yes, of course. I trotted to my car, hurrying because the poor thing was suffering so much. I came back and waved the wand over the dog, but nothing happened. It just kept crying and failing to stand, its tortured howls becoming deeper and more human. I waved the wand again. Still nothing. The magic had run out. There was nothing I could do. I walked back to my car to get the tire iron. ◆

CHARLIE PECK

PRONGHORN

Haven't driven in years, but if I slipped
behind the wheel of a four-door and spit out of town,

loosely west until the hills parted, and I could see only
flat earth, boundless sky, sure I'd think of you.

That long week we spent in the snow, in silence.
County access roads, highways split by ditch

and plastic-scrap wire. A gas pump and its analog numbers
rusted to a stop, forever $8.34. One bar so small

that our three beers and plate of cheese curds
the whole day's sale. Wautoma, Wisconsin,

knuckle of a town you picked at random, so we rented
a cabin on a frozen lake, brought the dog. Spent

every night in the hot tub, slipping into a gin
and brownie haze. At the Piggly Wiggly in town

we asked a manager for t-shirts, and she loved you
and your accent so much she nearly cried. Something

about the marquee next to the street, the setting sun
lighting puddles in the parking lot ablaze. And later

when you asked me if I'd move to Utah with you,
I remember looking through the windshield at a man

loading fishing gear into the bed of his truck, his son
holding open a steaming thermos between them,

a fog cloud that made the boy wince away. It was still dark
the morning you left and drove west, avoiding Nebraska,

three syllables of corn and cracked cement, the chain link
backstop behind home plate rattling in a storm.

Then that final weekend, in Wyoming, when we'd pulled
off the road and sat on the bumper, watching the hills

in twilight-relief on the horizon. You noticed them first, the animals
grazing in the valley. Not quite deer or gazelle, and neither

of us knew the name, and we vowed never to look, to leave them a mystery.
We sat there as dusk came on, the fruit stand sunset turning

their brown coats gold. One looked up, sniffed the damp air,
then leapt over the creek, behind the hills, gone.

MARIKA GUTHRIE

PRODIGAL FRIED CHICKEN

THE DARKEST MEAT is always the kind of oily that gets into the grooves of your fingers. That special type of greasy that leaves fingerprints on slick imitation leather, the tender skin of a cheek, the smudged glass of the inside of a Peterbilt passenger side window. All these particular sebaceous markers would one day lead to the satisfactory resolution of Sandra Valerie Roberts's murder as she was found with the balm of that final meal on her hands. Lorenzo Torres recounted to us that he told police he knew the girl wasn't sleeping. Not face down with no shoes tucked into a cholla patch with the rest of the trash blown in from Highway 40. Mr. Torres had stood respectfully at Sandy Roberts's bare feet and shook his head, but he had chickens to deliver. He didn't touch nothing except the road with his ostrich skin boots. When he got himself to a payphone, he called it in to New Mexico State Patrol. But we aren't going to talk about that disturbing event. Why would we venture into that gore and sadness when we can talk about Sandy when she was alive and decently beautiful and loved fried chicken.

SPITTING DISTANCE from Gallop, but on the Arizona side of the border, not quite to Chambers, lay an ARCO gas station. In the heartless light of that all-night stopover, Sandy lounged on the curb of the unused handicap parking spots. Her stonewashed Jordache jeans cut off so short that the lower curve of her ass touched the concrete, hot enough to cook eggs. Sandy wasn't cooking eggs, of course. No one but the Arizona D.A.R.E program bothered with such dribble. Sandy wasn't cooking eggs, but she was looking to sell her hot dish to anyone with twenty bucks or a ride over to the New Mexico side of life where *Mama Rita's Hen House* sat in a dirt lot on an access road that required the driver to loop back west for ¾ of mile on a strip of washboard rutted and bitchy enough to loosen whatever bad teeth might reside in the heads of those unfortunate enough to travel it.

IF ... *if* your ride made it to that two-toned single-wide trailer with an awning threadbare and low hanging as an old woman's favorite brassiere, then you would be anointed with fingers that had touched the tenebrous, bloody, devotional holy fat of chickens blessed to have ended their short lives on the sanguineous cottonwood stump of Mama Rita Ramirez. The woman's axe so sharp and her swing so flawless that never did the last pulses of their feathered hearts spatter her luminous white cotton blouse. The grain of the old stump absorbed every sin the hens' black eyes had ever seen. Without their heads the sassy birds had no say over what happened to their plump dry breasts, tight hard-angled wings, and bewitching, succulent, dark thighs. Plucked of their downy finery to the firm dimpled skin, the old girls were as indecent and available as any whore working a truck stop. Mama Rita just had this way of making them respectable in their plastic wicker beds with a folded blanket of coleslaw, fluffy biscuit pillow, and their nightgowns of breaded lace.

SANDY, in her stonewashed Jordache short shorts, thought about Mama Rita's chicken a lot. A borrowed cigarette, sometimes a Newport menthol and sometimes something as dull as a GPC, became a long drooping cinder arch when she fixated on Mama Rita's. Then the scalding asteroid of ash would land on her thigh, and Sandy would cuss and swat the offending mess off onto the span of asphalt that circled the ARCO, touched highway 40 and ran away from her in both directions. To the west Holbrook, Winslow, and Flagstaff—all places Sandy had been and had no desire to return to despite the formidable pines and the cooler days. We could dig up Sandy's past with two greedy hands. Greedy hands had been Sandy's trouble from about the time she could say *No, Uncle Leon.* But why would we want to reveal those dispiriting and privately violent times when we could talk about Sandy when she still had all her teeth and a forehead that was smooth and knuckles that did not crack open when she knocked on the doors of trucks parked at the ARCO.

TRAVELING EAST brought to Sandy's mind no distant trembling recollections. Her Jordache shorts hiked high enough to split her better sense into halves. Sandy traded ass for cash or ice or, if the driver was headed east, a ride to Mama Rita's for one of her respectable little beds of fried chicken. The sticky, goopy, and sometimes sour business dealt with, she would slump into the passenger seat in a soporific stupor. One driver told her she was about as good company as a bag of potato chips. Sandy, high as Laika the Russian-cosmonaut mongrel orbiting earth in 1957, had turned and observed the gray, hairy ear of the driver headed to the feed lots of Amarillo. She looked into that fleshy, crusty coil and saw the Fibonacci sequence, that universal fractal unfurling from its tight hook ... 1, 1, 2, 3, 5, 8, 13, 21 ... Sandy pressed her smooth-smooth forehead into the window glass. The erect chrome lock shone as the black top ran thick and relentless below. Her finger went into her mouth, a dry finger. Around that finger she muttered $s = ut + ½at^2$. *What the fuck you mumbling about?* The driver's own mouth was not quite a sphere circling his question. Sandy dragged her eyes away from the road and stared into that not-quite sphere of the driver's mouth. Euler's equation would make that man's face right. Sandy left her finger in her mouth, her tongue captivated by the tangibility of that appendage, and growled

$V - E + F = 2$. The driver pulled on the ear that Euclid defined, spit a tail of Red Man into a PBR can with a swallow-full of warm piss water in the bottom, and shook his head. *Next time girl, I'm leaving you at the damn ARCO.*

IF WE WERE CREATING a podcast about Sandy Valerie Roberts, we would be remiss to not interview Mr. Devereaux, her math teacher. To not sit in his neat, dim office at Coconino High and watch him tear up at the mention of her. Watch that man, enormous as a football coach but without that mean, meaty masculinity, straighten his name plaque while composing himself. He would tell us they had gotten Sandy a full-ride scholarship. He would tell us she was headed to MIT. He would tell us he almost got her out. Almost got her away from all those greedy-privately-violent hands. He would show us a photo of Sandy in a pair of shoes. But it would be impossible to interview Mr. Deveraux, who passed away from colon cancer in 1995. Besides, why would we want to discuss a grown man crying when we can talk about Sandy when she still remembered Coulomb's law, and could, even with her sinus cavities viscous with meth, calculate the amount of force between two electrically charged particles at rest.

SANDY CONCLUDED that she and *Mama Rita's Hen Hous*e were of opposite charges, though she wasn't sure which of them was positive and which negative, and what the fuck did it matter. What did matter was the power of the pull she felt at each mile marker post. What did matter was how Mama Rita took Sandy's sour, sticky money without comment. What did matter was the bit of shade the ripped awning offered over the solitary card table and three rusted dining chairs. What mattered was that meritorious plastic wicker basket, the paper hot from the fryer. What mattered was that after traveling through space and time, Sandy would not be able to bite into the baroque skin of those heavenly hens. Inside her stomach, Coulomb's law was in effect again. Sandy and the chicken repelled each other. The dark meat of the hen and the dark meat of the girl were ultimately homologous.

WE COULD DO A MONTAGE of photographs of Sandy to be accompanied by her favorite Depeche Mode song, "Personal Jesus." A meager collection of farinaceous color images that suggest she was susceptible to the flimsy lasso of a 35mm shutter and click. But why would we want to reduce Sandy down to cellulose triacetate, light sensitive gelatin emulsion, and an inattentive eye when we could talk about her when she was adjusting to walking barefoot after losing her last pair of shoes. Why would we frame her into that history when we could recall how Sandy tiptoed away from *Mama Rita's* toward the highway with its infinite pulsing projectiles of exodus, reminisce about the unguarded soles of her feet lifting the scintillating mica from the dirt as she tore the darkest meat from the bone, tossing it to the bankrupt mouths of feral dogs. Watch her wipe her fingers on those stonewashed Jordache cutoff shorts, sanctifying herself with the inescapable grease. ◆

CAITLYN KLUM

THIRD GRADE

Tommy enjoys drawing houses, but he will
quickly become frustrated at his lack

of fine motor skills and resort
to crossing out his work in a way

that is violent and concerning
until the whole page is filled

with harsh coils of black ink.
Today was a disaster on the swings.

Swing is a verb. But Liam says he hates
his body anyway, so he doesn't care

when they say bad things about him.
Once, I was able to help a girl

take off her coat for the first time.
Every day, Gabrielle wears the same Snow

White sweatshirt, which she drags through
her ketchup at lunch. Fiona is holding out a pair

of zigzag scissors during the unit
on biographies of famous figures.

When Fern heard a new low-fi song
my phone shuffled to, her life

changed instantly, and she began to wail.
Everyone has a job, and yours

is to erase all the pencil markings
on the spelling folders. Literally no one here

owns a horse. Yes, they do. No they don't.
Yes they do. No, not them.

I wish I could stay in the bathroom,
checking my face. What compromises

can we make with James so he doesn't
feel he has to bring a printout

photograph of a dog to PE? Boys
are not allowed to go to the bathroom.

Girls are not allowed to go to the bathroom
together. Girls always want to

push the teachers on the spinning metal
contraption in the playground, but they do not

understand it takes teachers a long time
to recover from that feeling. Now

I am teaching through laryngitis. Teacher,
what is a menace? I have done damage

to myself. There is only one of me
and seven of you. A boy named Tate

is afraid of beginnings. Something pathological
about indecisiveness and blah

blah. Everyone talks at once if you ask them
about the layout of their houses.

If you ask me, I also hate the art teacher
and hope they fire her. Zach can't be

allowed to rest his head on the carpet
during math. I write the date in bubble numbers

and stay late, standing like a bright flag
in the middle of the field.

SOO J. HONG

CLOSE CALL

1.

Janice watched the couple stumble into the tattoo parlor. They weren't holding hands. They were holding *bodies,* wedged so tight that the only way to get closer would be to bite each other. Teeth-on-skin, lip-on-flesh like suction cups. She listened to their sing-song yodel and the nasal valleys of the lovers' patois. *Mandarin.* Detecting the woman's soft diction topped with lispy peaks, Janice figured she was fresh-off-the-boat Taiwanese, and he was ABC—American Born Chinese.

Being neither but having spent the last eight months freelancing on Tuesday nights in Alhambra, Janice had seen some variation of the couple before. It was always heavy-set guys with the waifs. The men tanned as if they were working in rice fields and not selling SIM cards in the strip mall cell phone stores littering the east side; the women snow-white Asian Rapunzels living in the cocoon of a self-contained Chinese village in Los Angeles County, 6,000 miles from the mainland. *No English, no problem.*

Occasionally a white guy with yellow fever showed up oblivious to the tsk-tsk judgment from the 80-plus year-old grandmothers sitting at hostess stands in restaurants listed in hipster newsletters. Thanks to Taiwanese fan girls hot for HoriYen tattoos, Alhambra, a city of 80,000 just east of downtown, had become a mecca for ink and easy money for Janice Lee.

The two giggled in bursts trying to contain themselves, and then he picked up his date and twirled her around like a happy rag doll. She obliged, tilting her head back, her lilac and pear fragranced shampoo filling up the small storefront. When the China doll yelped, *"Wǒ qù"—oh, shit*—Janice pointed the drunk girl towards the bathroom.

While his date was in the bathroom, he paced the room until he turned and started to say something in Mandarin and Janice explained, "Sorry. I'm not Chinese."

"I knew it," he said, "Korean. Right?"

"Yeah. Do you know what you want?"

He hesitated then explained that the couple had connected online a month ago, and that she had flown in from Taiwan to meet in person.

"I didn't expect her to be so hot. All those bots, so I said, 'I'll get you a ticket, bring your ass to LA.' Now she says she's in love with me."

He started giggling again. Snorting out exhales from his wide fleshy nose. Janice tried hard not to roll her eyes or slap him straight across his flushed red-purple cheek. Or kick his grizzly bear belly. But she heard gagging from the bathroom, so instead she yelled out, "You okay in there?"

"She doesn't understand English," he said and winked.

"You're using my bathroom so she doesn't ruin your car. That's twenty bucks." Janice could see his white Porsche 911 convertible backed into the spot in front of the door, with its top down and a rear curvier than his date.

"Chill, Korea. She wants us to get tattoos to seal the deal," he said, and explained that she'd been in LA since Thursday morning and was scheduled to head back home late that night.

"Okay. There's the wall with the different styles. Not too big. And obviously no Tebori," Janice said, pointing to the wall framing the entrance with its three posters of calligraphic Hanzi, Hangul, and Kanji hung left to right—a pictogram of the Asian diaspora.

The entire parlor was the same glistening white and black as the Porsche, white high-gloss walls, black-trimmed windows, one black massage table. There were two barbershop chairs and a shampoo sink, homage to what had been the shop's previous incarnation. Janice's book, its cover the electric blue of an Yves Klein painting, gave the scene a jolt of color.

He didn't move toward the wall, instead shifting his weight from one foot to the other, while alternating looks to Janice and the ground.

"You need the bathroom, too?"

"Do you do temporary tattoos?"

"Like henna?"

"I mean where the ink fades. I saw it online."

"Yeah, I can do those." Janice rarely got these requests in this part of town; they typically came from self-proclaimed influencers at her westside base in Venice. Appointments made well in advance for the new ink that faded in a year's time, dissipated with equal parts metabolic energy and forgetting.

"I want you to do mine in that temporary ink, and hers permanent."

"What the fuck, dude," Janice said. "That's messed up. No, I'm not down. Besides, you know you still get the needle, right?"

"Yeah, I know. I'll pay extra. Like a lot extra," he said.

"It's a minimum of $150 per tattoo. So $300 and up. But for your fraud, it's a thousand each. Minimum. Cash only." She hoped he'd back down, that $2,000 in cash would sober him up to his douchery.

But Janice also thought about her student loan payments and that she couldn't bear to ask her parents again for help, risking another argument about how becoming a lawyer would erase the tragedy of their only child graduating from Berkeley to draw butterflies on strangers.

The door opened to the bathroom, and the girl's heels clacked with each step on the linoleum, and soon she wedged herself back into his embrace. She looked at Janice with furrowed brows and twirled her slim pointer finger with its hot-pink manicured talon around the parlor. Then she giggled before whispering something in his ear.

They began speaking in hushed voices escalating quickly to a honking staccato that sounded to Janice a little like sheep bleating. She looked at her tools and checked her phone before her ears trained to the girl saying *báipiáo*—cheap freeloader.

He said to Janice, "We're ready, but do you have any photos of your work? She wants to be sure that your work matches her style."

"You can tell her that if she wants a Chanel double-C logo, it's an extra thousand." Janice pointed to her portfolio and crossed her bare arms. Her own tattoos started and ended on her torso; there was still a part of her that wanted to wear sleeveless tops to her parents' church.

As the lovebirds flipped through the pages, they squealed in delight, then he said, "Holy shit. You're good. What are you doing here?"

"I should ask her the same," Janice said.

"Relax." He unfolded a wad of hundred-dollar-bills and counted out twenty onto the counter.

Janice put the bilingual consent forms out and said, "Listen, I'll do hers for free if you both do the temporary."

He looked at Janice quickly then completed the form in large block letters with his name: Larry Tsui. He slapped his driver's license on the counter, then pointed at the stack of bills and said, "Nope. The plan's the plan. $2,000. Count it, if you want." Then he began filling out the form for his date, her name: Ming-Mei Wang.

"She's got to fill it out herself," Janice insisted. If Ming-Mei filled it out, it was consensual.

"Why you gotta be so uptight? She's not going to sue you."

Janice pushed the form towards Ming-Mei, who obliged and completed the paperwork. Janice said, "I need to see your passport."

Ming-Mei giggled as she handed Janice the EVA Airways boarding pass for her flight to Taipei and said, "Call me Minnie."

AS SHE DREW the monogram out on Minnie's wrist, Janice noticed a faint trace of a "P+M" where wrist met palm. Undetectable to a civilian, but Janice knew it in an instant: old ink lasered off. Minnie had been branded before.

Yet Minnie's flesh was as smooth as the practice sheets Janice used while apprenticing in Oakland. No matter what they said about the silicone being just like human flesh, the first time Janice put her pen on someone's actual arm, she realized the marketing was utter bullshit. Nothing was the same as making someone bleed.

"Is this Taylor Swift? Fucking girl music," Larry said, while he held Minnie's hand on the other side of the barber chair. He had started chewing gum and blew and snapped bubbles. Every once in a while a bubble popped, leaving a film of white elastic around his mouth.

Janice thought about letting Larry know that Taylor Swift's girl music had generated five billion dollars for the economy. Instead, she kept poking through the scarlet rivulets and black ink pooling on Minnie's snow-white canvas.

Once finished, Larry translated Janice's after-care instructions and confirmed he'd keep an eye on it for any sign of infection. Neither tattoo looked angry. Janice gave them the Mandarin language after-care instructions and threw in a complimentary magic balm. A part of Janice was annoyed that she was bearing witness to this two-way deceit; another part felt free. Let the two of them believe whatever they wanted. It was an easy $2,000.

SHE'D MET HER self-imposed nightly quota, and after the couple left, Janice closed up and began the drive to her parents' in Burbank where she'd been living since returning to LA.

During the drive, her thoughts alternated between Larry and her ex-boyfriend Vahe. Larry's spiked hair reminded her of Vahe's blue-black fade with a mop full of pomade on top.

She remembered the first night that she and Vahe spent together. Second semester freshman year, right before midterms. They'd grabbed a bag of tacos from Sinaloa then headed to his dorm room in Blackwell. He poured out tequila shots, and as she licked the salt off his neck, Janice smelled a mix of cardamom and sweat on his collarbone.

By 8 p.m., they were sitting at War Horse for an appointment he'd booked. Electricity pulsed in her legs as Vahe flashed his upper left arm, a tree of life and roots spreading down to his elbow. He explained it was his third and final visit, to have some of the roots extended to his wrist.

Encouraging Janice to get her own, Vahe offered, "My treat, and I'll hold your hand the entire time."

"I'm not ready to have something on me for the rest of my life," she said.

"What you resist persists. It won't hurt. Just a little pinching."

An hour later, Janice had her first tattoo: a small arrow, under her left breast. Vahe was still in his chair when Janice got her ink, and it hurt like hell. But she said nothing, instead biting the side of her tongue to imagine herself elsewhere.

They went to War Horse four more times, and a year later when they discovered Aristophanes's speech on other halves, Janice was apprenticing. She inked their matching *OH* monogram blocks adorning their belly buttons, and Janice knew she would never shake the thrill of shaving the hair above Vahe's navel to prepare his tattoo.

They'd met in Drawing Foundations, a class Janice told her parents was a graduation requirement. Eventually her transcript filled with Arts Practice classes coupled with those for an econ major, placating her parents. It was a mirror of Vahe's, their left-brain right-brain connection the roadmap to building a life.

"I can be the banker, and you can be an artist," Vahe said as they lay in bed at the start of senior year. It was a particularly hot September night, and they'd left the window open, hoping for a breeze to cut the stifling humidity. He traced his finger up and down her nose, his touch light and comforting.

"How come you are THE and I'm AN? Why are you definite and specific versus indefinite and general? And why can't I be *the* banker?" Janice asked, inflecting her tone up.

"Maybe you should have been an English major," Vahe said and brought his finger down to her lips. He kissed her, ending the conversation.

The next week, when job interview schedules were published, the companies on Janice's roster took both by surprise. JPMorgan, BCG, Google. Vahe's was thin with no prestige employer in the ranks. He was waitlisted for an interview with Deloitte, the second-tier firm a consolation prize.

"Did you apply for these?" he asked.

"I didn't. I swear."

"They need women, I guess."

Vahe picked up his things and left while Janice logged into the recruiting portal and declined the interviews. The following week Vahe interviewed with Deloitte and received a polite rejection, ending his plans to escape his family's business.

PASSING THE RAIL TRACKS at the 110 interchange, Janice saw signs for Atwater Village and exited. She made the left turn before Costco and parked in front of the house that Vahe now shared with roommates she did not know. One of his family's rental properties, the one he'd taken her to when it was between tenants the summer before their junior year. Where they'd made love on the hardwood floors with fresh paint on the walls and in Vahe's hair and on his knuckles, the acidic drying paint smell that she now thought of when masturbating.

The lights were on. Vahe's truck was parked in the driveway. Janice had heard that he had a new girlfriend, had seen a photo of them posted on Instagram.

She opened her phone and sent a text to Vahe. *How's it going?*

A few minutes passed, then finally his reply. *All good.*

She felt a rushing dizziness and quickly fired off, *How's the job search?*

As she thought about what else to write, Vahe's reply landed. *I can see your car on the street. Stop stalking me. I'm done.*

She replied *Ok,* but it sat there—a lone green bubble in a sea of blue bubbles. Blocked.

Janice turned on the engine and began her retreat. When she got to Los Feliz Boulevard, she turned left and the Tam O'Shanter came into view, its Tudor-style roof illuminated by the late summer's gloaming. She pulled into the parking lot and let the car idle while she opened the glove compartment.

Inside was a copy of Dorianne Laux's *What We Carry,* which she'd picked up at the Rose Bowl Flea months before. While the empty and lonely room on the cover had drawn her in, the poet's stark words captured Janice first as a prisoner, then an eternal jailbird failing recidivism. She'd memorized each poem, line by line, but the ritual of holding the book, turning its pages became a form of therapy.

Opening the book, she landed on "This Close," and the words nearly lifted her out of the car: *Wherever our bodies touch, the flesh comes alive.*

Reading further, Janice realized her inevitable destination that night. Pulling out of the parking lot, she gripped the wheel just a bit tighter and shook her head. Janice wanted to be as alert as possible when she arrived at the airport to confront Larry and Minnie.

THE INTERNATIONAL TERMINAL gleamed bright and clinical, the light-green-yellow film from the LED lights casting an alien glow.

Janice scanned the monitor to check details for the flight to Taipei: 12:05 a.m. on-time departure in just three hours. A prickly heat rose in her cheeks. Heading toward the counter for EVA check-in, she thought about what she'd say to Minnie. Tell her that Larry's tattoo wasn't permanent. Whatever he had promised, he'd wash himself clean once her flight took off. Or at the very least, it would fade ugly and in bits, the way first-love did. She'd tell Minnie that Larry was no conquest.

Rounding a corner, she saw the couple settled into an embrace. They weren't giggling any longer. They stood there with their foreheads pressed together, every few seconds pulling back and glancing at each other.

Janice held her distance though only a few paces in order to see Larry's face. She wouldn't let herself believe it, yet there he was. Larry was crying. Full sobs. Red, scrunched, cry-baby face.

2.

Larry felt like an ass. No-money, fat fuck that he was. There was no way the Taiwanese mannequin was ever going to be back in his arms. So, what did it matter that he cried? Sobbed in front of her. That was the silver lining to the impermanence, and he was letting it rip.

He could still feel the eyes of the woman at the check-in counter sizing him up and down. Larry had laid the keys to the Porsche with its shiny logo keychain on the counter. Minnie had looked at him with admiration, with those sultry eyes, her feathery long lashes batting, the agent's Mandarin lilting with deference as she checked Minnie in. Larry made a point of giving Minnie a wad of twenties—fifty of them—in front of the agent, encouraging Minnie to get something nice to eat inside the terminal. He winked at the agent, who nodded her approval.

Afterwards, they stood a few yards from the TSA entrance and held each other. Larry tasted the hint of Minnie's grape bubble gum from their last kiss. He could smell her fruity scent, and it hit him hard. He wanted to tell her that she should stay. But where? Live with him in his room at his mom's? Drive around in his twelve-year-old RAV4 after he'd returned the Porsche he'd borrowed from his boss? Get her a job as a server at Chengdu Taste?

Larry thought about buying a one-way ticket to Taipei. He had about $2,000 left in savings after the money he'd spent over the weekend with Minnie. The money that his grandfather had left him to pay tuition at PCC, rent his first apartment. What would he do with an associate's degree anyway?

They were starting to push timing to her gate, and Larry knew they'd have to say their goodbyes. He began holding her tighter, though he could feel her embrace getting looser, her tears waning.

"Fàngxīn. Dōu méiguānxì de," she cooed, to which he simply thought, *it will not be fucking okay. Not even close.*

Minnie pulled away and touched his chin. She grabbed his left hand and began walking to the TSA checkpoint. At the roped off entrance, she pulled her hand out of his, and with a final sigh-giggle, she cocked her head and said, "Good time for us." She made a peace sign and then walked toward the security lines. She didn't look back at Larry, who watched her until she disappeared into a sea of travelers.

RATHER THAN LEAVE THE AIRPORT, Larry sat at the bar in Planet Hollywood, scrolling through his phone. There was still a part of him that believed that he'd look up to find Minnie walking towards him. In this alternate version of the evening, she'd call out to him saying that she'd changed her mind. He looked at the photos from the weekend, zooming in on Minnie's moon-shaped face, her plush raspberry-gloss lips. Larry studied each photo as if they held a secret roadmap back to the weekend.

The only other time that he could remember feeling this type of sensation was in middle school when Sangeeta Patel had been his lab partner in eighth grade. They'd ended up sitting next to each other at their black countertop island, a result of both arriving last after lunch period on the first day. He hadn't known the word *serendipity* at the time, and years later upon discovering it in sophomore English, he'd say the word over and over, rolling its five syllables around on his tongue. Serendipity. *Sangeeta Patel.*

That semester the heat had lived up to the threat of a Santa Ana October, and during the entire twenty-two minutes of lunch, Larry would worry about the sweat stains in his armpits and that his hair looked as if he'd stepped out of a shower. But not once had Sangeeta scooted her chair away from his. Smelling like vanilla, she would flash a tender smile and say nothing when their scalpels touched during dissection. Then upon return from winter break, Larry entered biology to find Sangeeta's seat empty for the remainder of the year.

As he took a sip of whiskey, Larry experienced his karmic miasma: burning love, then emptiness. Again he sat next to an empty chair. Larry stared at the wrap on his wrist and wondered if he should have gone ahead with a permanent tattoo. To prove that the weekend had been real. But he'd thought better of it. People would eventually ask about its origin. That's what people do about tattoos, right? People want stories. Then what would he say?

He opened Instagram and went to the message section. He sent a heart emoji to Minnie. She would be at the gate. The message indicated *seen,* and Larry waited.

Then, what he'd dreaded since the first time connecting with Minnie on the app. Her profile went gray, her beautiful photo rendered blank with a faceless icon, wiping out any trace of Minnie's presence in his life. *Ghosted.* She would now forever be his *jiǔwěihú,* the nine-tailed fox that seduced then consumed Larry whole, the shapeshifting creature from his grandfather's fables a myth no more.

His head was still down, his eyes fixed on the photos when the barstool next to him scraped concrete, and a woman's voice asked, "What are you crying about?" Her tone sounded accusatory yet familiar.

Larry turned and saw the tattoo girl from Alhambra. For a split second he struggled to place her. Where had she come from?

She sat down, put her keys on the bar and gestured to the bartender.

"What the fuck, Korea? Who said anything about crying?" The last sentence stuck in his throat as he pushed the words out. How did she know he had been crying? Were his eyes swollen?

"You following me?"

"Not exactly," she said. "I wanted to tell Minnie that you lied, that your tattoo isn't permanent."

"What?" Larry tried to make sense of her words. "Who the fuck made you God?" His face was hot with fury.

"I didn't. I saw you guys, and well," she hesitated, "you got yours." Her words hung in the air while she ordered her drink.

"What the fuck does that mean?" Larry asked.

"She ghost you?"

While the humiliation coursed through his body, the girl continued. Something about lasers and cosmetic tattoo removal, about it not being Minnie's first.

"How much she get you for?" she asked. "At least $2,000 with me."

Larry stood up. His rage quickly morphed into disbelief then a feeling he'd grown to know too well: shame. He slumped into his seat, put his head in his hands. He felt sobs rising, but gulped air to keep them down.

"Whoa. Shit. I'm sorry," she said, and they sat there for a few minutes while Larry practiced box-breathing.

Feeling his face cool down, he blinked hard and turned to the girl and said, "Come on, Korea, it's cool. You think I don't know about that hustle?"

Silence, then finally she said, "Listen, I'm sorry. I thought you knew. You seemed not to care all that much before. It's all fun and games, right?"

"Yup, you get it," Larry said, "You hungry?" The girl looked as surprised as Larry felt, but she shrugged and studied the menu.

"Get whatever you want. That kind of night. What's your name, Korea?"

"Janice Lee," she said as the bartender took their orders.

While waiting for their meal, they traded abridged versions of their lives. Initially, Janice seemed determined to find some flaw. What did he do for a living: manager at a uniform supply company for hotels. Favorite food: fried chicken. At first, Larry resisted her questions, but she'd suggested a game of two truths and a lie and offered hers first: speaks fluent Italian; afraid of latex balloons; has one kidney. When it turned out that she didn't speak fluent Italian, some part of Larry shifted, melting like a pad of butter left out on the table.

He gave his: dad killed in a car accident when he was three; never had wisdom teeth; allergic to nuts. She snorted and shouted at him, "No way a Chinese guy is allergic to nuts!"

They laughed and then Janice announced, "Drove my dad home from jail after he got arrested for beating me and my mom; hate Ranch dressing; thought I was going to be a lawyer."

"Really?" Larry asked, knowing that the salad dressing was the lie. She'd polished off her Ranch chicken entrée, asking for extra dressing on the side.

He felt a rush he hadn't experienced with Minnie. "Lawyer. Makes a lot of sense," he said, raising his glass of whiskey. Janice met his toast, and finishing, slammed her glass onto the bar.

Eventually, they discovered they'd gone to school just fifteen miles from each other and had been at the same football playoff game as high school seniors when Janice's Burbank Bulldogs defeated Larry's Alhambra Moors. She in her cheerleading uniform waving tinsel pom-poms; he in his jersey, benched with a season-ending knee injury ending any chance of playing tight end as a walk-on at PCC. Fifteen miles to fifty yards had separated them then as they cheered from respective sidelines. Now they sat at an airport bar, the divide closing.

After dessert and another round of drinks, Larry felt loose and asked, "You ever been in love?" He reasoned that it wasn't too much to ask after a girl tells you her dad hit her.

"Maybe. Or what I thought was love," Janice said. "But what do I know? I guess I know more about what love isn't." Her words then came out slow and labored, "You were branding her, Larry. You can't just do that to a woman."

It was as if she'd slapped him, a wake-up call from the lugubrious glaze of the two cocktails and steak dinner. *What he'd done to Minnie? What he'd done to women?* It felt as if all the lights in the terminal were trained on him after entering through a stage door by mistake.

"*You* branded her," he whispered, then his words sped out like hot bullets, "You saw her laser shit. *Consensual. Two. Way. Transaction.*"

His insides coiled up and bounced to his throat like a wire spring. He wanted to shake Janice, to make her understand. That he wasn't a predator, but the prey. That he was looking for connection, and his only means was playing sugar daddy to a Taiwanese hustler. That he'd asked for the temporary ink to forget the shame of it sooner. That what Janice had done was spare him grief and should be proud of it. Rather, she was pouring scalding hot salt on his wounded heart. He wanted to beat his chest where it was thumping hardest, but he saw the side-eye glance of a server standing at the other end of the bar, so instead Larry stood up, motioning to the bartender to close his tab. Janice took out two hundred-dollar bills and placed them on the counter. Larry turned and walked, and soon he heard her calling, "Wait ... wait ..."

He hurried towards the exit, but she was next to him like a swarm of gnats. She grabbed his right arm, and he yanked it from her. "I don't know what you want but leave me the fuck alone."

Then suddenly, Janice pulled a rolled-up wad of bills out of her pocket and waved them like a shaman burning sage. "Here. You can have it back. Less two hundred."

"What?" Larry asked like he was re-engaging with a feral cat who'd scratched him.

"Because you don't need to use this," she said as she led him to a row of empty seats.

Once seated, Janice lowered her eyes and said, "God comes to your window, all bright light and black wings, and you're just too tired to open it."

Then raising her eyes to meet Larry's, Janice announced, "That's from Dorianne Laux's poem 'Dust.' Don't be so ashamed. Don't be so afraid of your life, Larry. We just spent three hours together and not once did you have to pay me to stay."

Words failed him, though a sweet taste returned to his mouth.

Finally, he blurted, "Why keep two hundred?"

"Three hundred for the tattoos, less one hundred for my share of dinner. So, we're square," she said with a sheepish grin. "I believe in karma."

Seeing Janice smile, Sangeeta Patel crossed his mind. Larry finally understood what Janice was offering. *Mercy.*

Without hesitation, he kissed the top of Janice's head, stood and ran towards the exit.

3.

Watching Larry race away, she felt a part of her release. First in her chest, a ball wound tight unraveling like loose string. She had been clenching both fists, one around the clumsy bouquet of cash and the other in her pocket. While she'd meant to soothe Larry, as he disappeared, she felt herself come back to life.

She stood and slowly spun around surveying the terminal, her hands raised above her head, her right hand still holding the roll of bills. There were no visible changes—same lighting, same din of white noise of passengers though fewer in number than before—but there was a rhythm. An ebb and flow.

At that moment, Janice recognized that the airport carried the full spectrum of human longing. On this departures level, there was ambivalence, crying. Downstairs, the reunited might signal joy, maybe even relief. On any given day, life pushed you towards the departure gate or baggage claim. Willingly or not.

Next to where she and Larry sat, an old Asian woman with snow-white hair slicked back cradled a sleeping toddler boy. The old woman began singing a lullaby in Chinese at full voice as if the terminal was empty. It sounded sad, though it could have been about anything. When their eyes locked, the lady smiled a toothless approval.

Janice called to the old woman, *"Měilì de,"* a Mandarin onomatopoeia, a word that sounded like "melody," a word that her clients often said at a session's end, staring down at their bloodied wound. *Měilì de.* Beautiful. ◆

KATEY FUNDERBURGH

I'VE BEEN A CHILD

before, at the river's
edge where I made my-
self naked. Cricket-thick
night unfurled above
me. Lather in the algae.
Sundress like a pelt
on the shore. A girl
before her hipbones
rounded like the bowl made
by a forehead pressed
into the mud
where the cattails
grew dense. I took
a bar of soap
to my unfurred
skin and let
my river cover, enter
me. Before I felt
the slits of eyes
on the birthmarks
on the backs
of my legs like I'd always
been capable
of blood. Even
my river caught
tampon wrappers
in the barbed wire
rusted and washed down
to her cypress grove.
After that I kept
my swimsuit on, ran

the bar of soap underneath
my seams, submerged my uncut
braids and cupped
my hands to carry
water up to my
bikini top, hoped
it'd soak through
to the skin of my chest.
If there
is a wolf there
I've done anything but
put her down. Sucked
the water from my fingers
like marrow. Bluestem
grass grew wrist-high
and over the hills the hawks
stained their beaks
with roadkill, fed
their children with it.

FROM THE PUBLISHER

TO EVERYONE now holding this issue,

It has been a long road as we are addressing some concerns we have for our magazine's place in this world. Our concerns are most often answered thanks to our collective resourcefulness, generosity, know-how, and ethics.

Thanks to us paying close attention to the good being done elsewhere, *Raleigh Review* is now nationally distributed through Fernwood Press in Oregon to over fifty bookshops. Also, our magazine now has avenues for discounts via Ingram from global booksellers such as Thrift Books, Barnes & Noble, Powell's, Blackwells (UK), Yes24 (Korea) and Amazon most anyplace. We hope you enjoy this one, as our magazine speaks best through the works we publish. We believe art should challenge as well as entertain. You can now find our magazine in many places throughout the lands, both online and inside these fine bookshops and newsstands:

Village Works NYC
New York, NY 10003

Codex Books
New York, NY 10012

Iconic Magazines
New York, NY 10012

Casa Iconic Magazines
New York, NY 10014

Milkweed Editions
Minneapolis, MN 55415

Brewery Bhavana
Raleigh, NC 27601

Quail Ridge Books
Raleigh NC 27609

Literary Arts
Portland OR 97214

The Homer Bookstore
Homer AK 99603

The NewSouth Bookstore
Montgomery AL 36104

Pyramid Art,
Books and Framing
Little Rock AR 72206

The Scribbled Hollow
Glendale AZ 85301

La Playa Books
San Diego CA 92106

Revolution Books
Berkeley CA 94704

Underground Books
Sacramento CA 95817

Westside Stories
Colorado Springs CO 80905

Possible Futures
New Haven CT 06511

Bridge Street Books
Washington DC 20007

Books & Books
Coral Gables FL 33134

Pilsen Community Books
Chicago IL 60608

Schimmel's Bookery
Bowling Green KY 42101

Lunar and Lake Book Market
Fond du Lac WI 54935

Arundel Books
Seattle WA 98104

BookTree
Kirkland WA 98033

Antidote Books
Brattleboro VT 05301

The Book Nook
Ludlow VT 05149

Basket Books & Art
Houston TX 77006

Deep Vellum Books
Dallas TX 75226

DDR Books
Watertown SD 57201

Bindlestiff Books
Philadelphia PA 19143

White Whale Bookstore
Pittsburgh PA 15224

Lost Avenue Books
Portland OR 97217

Downbound Books
Cincinnati OH 45223

Gramercy Books
Bexley OH 43209

Collected Works Bookstore &

Coffeehouse
Santa Fe NM 87501

Sheafe Street Books
Portsmouth NH 03801

The King's English Bookshop
Salt Lake City UT 84105

Arts & Letters Bookstore
Granbury TX 76048

Literati Bookstore
Ann Arbor MI 48104

Blue Hill Books
Blue Hill ME 04614

Gulf of Maine Books
Brunswick ME 04011

Owl & Turtle Bookshop
Camden ME 04843

Viva Books
Baltimore MD 21201

Amherst Books
Amherst MA 01002

Grolier Poetry Book Shop
Cambridge MA 02138

Scuppernong Books
Greensboro NC 27401

Turnsol Books
Kansas City MO 64108

Yellow Dog Bookshop
Columbia MO 65201

. . . more to be added.

Rob Greene, publisher

contributors

SEAN CHO A. is a writer living in the Southern United States.

COLLEEN BARAN is a queer, disabled writer from Canada. Her work has appeared in *Pleiades*, *Magma*, *Berkeley Poetry Review*, *PRISM*, and the anthology *Best Canadian Poetry*. She has won poetry and flash fiction awards from *PRISM* and *Magma*.

ELIZABETH ROSE BRUCE is a poet from Chattanooga, Tennessee. They hold an MFA from UNC Greensboro where they were Poetry Editor of *The Greensboro Review*. Liz's work has been featured or is forthcoming in *Southern Humanities Review*, *Poetry South*, and *Arkana*, and anthologized in *Objects in this Mirror* (Press 53).

LUCAS CARDONA is visiting assistant professor of English at McMurry University in Abilene, Texas. He holds an MFA in poetry from University of North Carolina Wilmington. His poetry has appeared or is forthcoming in *The Threepenny Review*, *Birmingham Poetry Review*, *The Greensboro Review*, *New Ohio Review*, *wildness*, and *The Shore*.

ABIGAIL CLOUD is editor-in-chief of *Mid-American Review* and teaches at Bowling Green State University. Her first collection, *Sylph* (Pleiades, 2014) was a winner of the Lena-Miles Wever Todd Prize. Other work has appeared in publications such as *South Dakota Review*, *Cincinnati Review*, and *Tupelo Quarterly*.

ASHLEY W. CUNDIFF is a musician and writer of essays and fiction. Her work has appeared in numerous publications, most recently *Novellum* and *Swing*, and she is a reader for *Wild Roof Journal*. Ashley lives in Virginia with her family and can be found at ashleywcundiff.substack.com and thedomesticwilds.com.

KATEY FUNDERBURGH (she/her) is a queer Colorado poet. She is a current MFA candidate at George Mason University, where she also teaches literature and creative writing courses. Katey is the co-coordinator of the Incarcerated Writers Project of *Phoebe Journal*, and is a Poetry Alive! program manager and teaching fellow. Some of her work is published or forthcoming in *Best New Poets 2025* and *The Rumpus*.

MARIKA GUTHRIE is an emerging writer residing in Pueblo, Colorado. She is a nontraditional undergraduate attending CSU-Pueblo. Marika is an ardent horsewoman, a stumbling philosopher, and poet. She has published in *The Baltimore Review*, *The New Ohio Review*, *The Rappahannock Review*, *The Blue Mesa Review*, *La Piccioletta Barca*, *Tempered Steele*, and *Vortex*. Her work will be featured in *The McNeese Review* in spring of 2026.

MILLY HELLER lives in New Orleans. Her short fiction appears in *Fiction Attic Press*, *Tangled Locks*, *Parhelion*, *RavensPerch*, and millyheller.com.

SOO J. HONG'S fiction can be found in *Chicago Quarterly Review* and *Narrative*. A recent finalist for the *Iowa Review* Award and shortlisted for the *StoryQuarterly* prize, Soo is an alumna of Community of Writers and Bread Loaf Writers' Conference. Her work has received support from PEN America Emerging Voices.

CAITLYN KLUM'S poems appear in *The Los Angeles Review of Books Quarterly Journal*, *Four Way Review*, *American Chordata*, and others. A graduate of the Michener Center for Writers, she is currently a PhD student in English and Literary Arts at the University of Denver.

ABBY MANZELLA is the author of *Ripples into the Wild* (Cornerstone Press 2027), in which this story will appear, and *Migrating Fictions: Gender, Race, and Citizenship in U.S. Internal Displacements*, winner of the SSAWW Book Award. A 2025 Pushcart Prize winner, she has published with *The Threepenny Review*, *Massachusetts Review*, and *Pleiades*.

RILEY MAYES is a writer from Portland, Maine. She obtained her Master's in English Literature from the University of Edinburgh. Her creative work has been published in various journals, including *Platform Review, Mantis, The Portland Press Herald, Anthroposphere,* and others. When she's not writing, she loves hiking, running, reading, and nosing about in the woods.

ABHISHEK MEHTA is a marketing professional from India with a passion for putting words together. His writing has previously appeared and is forthcoming in *Prairie Schooner, South Dakota Review, Dunes Review, Clackamas Literary Review* and more.

JEREMIAH MORIARTY is a writer from Minneapolis. His poems and stories have appeared in *The Rumpus, Strange Horizons, swamp pink, Diode, The Cortland Review,* and elsewhere. Additionally, his writing has been nominated for a Pushcart Prize, the PEN/Robert J. Dau Prize, and Best of the Net.

CHARLIE PECK is from Omaha, Nebraska. His poetry has appeared or is forthcoming in *Indiana Review, The Journal, Ninth Letter,* and *POETRY*, among others. His first collection, *World's Largest Ball of Paint* (2024), received the 2022 St. Lawrence Book Award from Black Lawrence Press.

RYAN PEED is a fiction writer from Kyle, Texas. He holds a degree in Exercise and Sports Science from Texas State University. An MFA student at the University of Houston, his fiction appears or is forthcoming in *Southeast Review, MoonPark Review, Jet Fuel Review, Cutleaf Journal,* and *Raleigh Review.*

Poems by REBECCA PYLE recently appear in *The Hiram Poetry Review*, *Anacapa Review*, and *Eclectica*; essays, fiction, and visual art by her appear in many more art/lit journals and reviews. After spending two years in Europe searching for the most perfect viennois she is now living in northern New Mexico. See rebeccapyleartist.com.

BEN REED teaches in the English Department at Texas State University. He lives in Austin, where he is at work on a novel about memory and IKEA. "My Turn with the Wand" was written after a short stay in Alameda, California.

ELIZABETH ROSEN (she/her) is a native New Orleanian and a transplant to small-town Pennsylvania. She misses gulf oysters and Southern ghost stories but has become appreciative of snow and colorful scarves. She mourns the loss of Tab and still wants her MTV. Learn more at www.thewritelifeliz.com.

RODRIGO SCHÖNARDIE is Brazilian and writes in both English and Portuguese. Currently living in France with his Irish husband, he works as a university language teacher. His stories have been published in Brazil, France, the USA, and Ireland, and he is now seeking representation for his first novel in English.

MATTHEW J. SPIRENG'S 2019 Sinclair Poetry Prize-winning book *Good Work* was published by *Evening Street Press*. A 13-time Pushcart Prize nominee, he is the author of two other full-length poetry books, *What Focus Is* and *Out of Body,* winner of the 2004 Bluestem Poetry Award, and five chapbooks. Website: matthewjspireng.com.

contributors cont.

TAYLOR STONEMAN is a painter and poet living in Northern California, where she is a Root Division Studio Artist. Her debut solo exhibition, *Earthbody,* took place at MADSEN Gallery last fall; her second solo show, Mother Desert, opens at Root Division in spring 2026. She has completed a residency at Vermont Studio Center and been featured in *Suboart Magazine.*

CLAIRE MARIE TORN is a New York writer, actor, and filmmaker. She created two series: *Rent Control* (Vimeo) and *Amateur City* (Relay, Filmzie). Her short stories, "Sugar Baby" and "Profile 9204," are in anthologies by Outcast Press under her former pen name CT Marie. This is her first piece published under her real name.

DOMINIC VITI is the author of *Broken: Bits and Pieces* (Cornerstone Press, 2027). His short stories appear in *Chorus* (Simon & Schuster), *Harvard Review*, and *Beloit Fiction Journal*, among others. His work as a copywriter has won the Cannes Lion, Effie, Webby, and Telly awards. He lives in Colorado.

WENDY WISNER is the author of three books of poems, most recently *The New Life,* published by Cornerstone Press and named a finalist for the Foreword INDIES Book of the Year. Wendy's poems have appeared in *Alaska Quarterly Review, Prairie Schooner, Spoon River Review, Passages North*, and elsewhere.

NELLE YVON lives in Georgia with her family and writes poems about the doomsday cult of her youth. Nelle is the managing editor for *Beyond Bars*, a literary journal that amplifies the voices of incarcerated writers. Her poetry can be found in *Tulsa Review, Birdcoat Quarterly*, and *Defunkt Magazine.*

LUCY ZHANG writes, codes, and watches anime. Her work has appeared in *Flash Frog, Virginia Quarterly Review, Shenandoah, The Massachusetts Review*, and elsewhere. Find her at https://lucyzhang.tech.

YAN ZHANG is a student currently residing in Hangzhou, China. Her work has appeared or is forthcoming in *Sierra Nevada Review, The Shore*, and *Shō Poetry Journal,* among others. She enjoys matcha lattes, taking long strolls in her neighborhood, observing the changing colors of leaves, and thinking.

www.ingramcontent.com/pod-product-compliance
Lightning Source LLC
LaVergne TN
LVHW052354100826
845147LV00013B/840

* 9 7 8 1 5 9 4 9 8 2 2 9 3 *